The Red
Wind

The Red Wind

Wind

Sarah M. Traylor

ABINGDON   NASHVILLE

THE RED WIND

Copyright © 1977 by Abingdon

All rights reserved.

Library of Congress Cataloging in Publication Data

TRAYLOR, SARAH M   1908—
  The red wind.

  SUMMARY: Seeking his fortune in Charles Town,
South Carolina in 1759, Angus Ferguson finds his life
threatened and flees to Fort Loudoun, an English
outpost in Cherokee country, where he encounters
even further danger.
  [1. United States—History—Colonial period, ca.
1600-1775—Fiction] I. Title.
PZ7.T6892Re   [Fic]   77-3532

ISBN 0-687-35881-7

MANUFACTURED BY THE PARTHENON PRESS AT
NASHVILLE, TENNESSEE, UNITED STATES OF AMERICA

For
Susan and Kerry

Contents

VIRGINIA

NORTH CAROLINA

● FORT LOUDOUN

Nuquasee●

———FORT PRINCE GEORGE

The Red
Wind

0   50   100

Trading Paths ----

GEORGIA

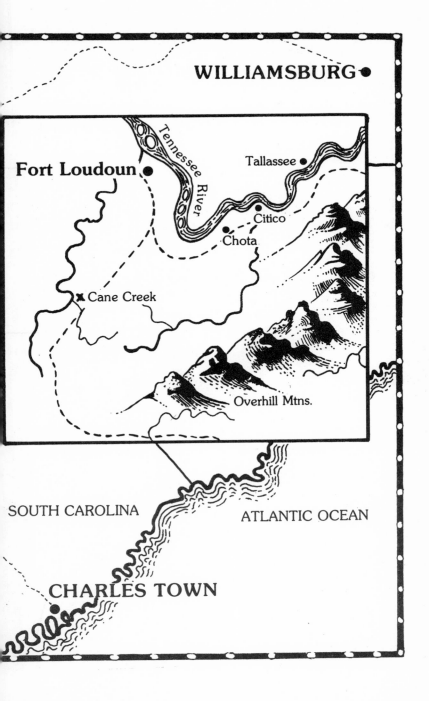

WILLIAMSBURG •

Fort Loudoun •

Tennessee River

Tallassee •

Citico

Chota

✕ Cane Creek

Overhill Mtns.

SOUTH CAROLINA

ATLANTIC OCEAN

CHARLES TOWN •

Prologue

It lies before me now as I write—a small round thing of silver—the king's medallion. It has the face of the English king on one side and on the other a motto, "Evil to him who evil thinks"—a proud face and a proud motto.

It was once a gift from that king to the little chief, Attakullakulla, treasured by him above all honors. How it came to my hand is a strange story, but Captain Stuart wishes me to write it from the beginning.

1
The Slaver

It was late in the afternoon of August 12, 1759, that we sighted the slaver.

I can never forget the exact date of that affair, for to it and to the consequent happenings I owed a sharp change in my prospects as a young man out to make my way in the new world of the Carolinas.

"Ship to larboard!" called the lookout above us.

All on the deck of our ship, *The Wanderer,* six weeks out of Glasgow, rushed to the rail, peering through the scudding clouds of intermittent showers.

"What ship?" the captain called. "Frenchman or pirate?"

We held tense for the answer. In either case we were in for trouble—and we were only two days out of Charles Town, our destination.

"Neither, sir!" came the answer, and we breathed easier. *"The Indian Queen."*

Then we saw her in a brief burst of sunlight—a West Indiaman, low and spare, built for one thing—speed.

"The devil's own! She's carrying slaves," growled the mate standing next to me at the rail. "She can show her heels to anything on the seven seas."

"She's beautiful," I said, admiring the lean lines of the speeding ship, even now drawing away from us.

"Ye wouldn't think so, young sir, if ye was downwind of her. The stench would turn ye stomach!"

"How many slaves does she hold?"

11

"The Lord only knows—as many as can be crowded on. They sleep spoon-fashion if they sleep at all."

A chill went down my spine. We were crowded enough on *The Wanderer*—but spoon-fashion!

"You know a lot about slavers," I remarked. "Have you ever shipped on one?"

The mate turned his attention to me. He scowled and spat.

"I'm a God-fearin' man, sir! I ain't sunk so low. Frenchmen, pirates, and slavers—Lord save us from such!"

We watched, secure in the thought of our own safety, as the distance grew.

Suddenly the lookout yelled from his elevated perch. All eyes turned to watch him. He yelled again, "She's throwing 'em overboard!"

A collective gasp went up. The captain, at his station above us, swung his glass to his eye. I leaped on a coil of rope, and I could see what was visible to the lookout and the captain—objects swarming in the wake of the ship. By that time the crew and many of the passengers had leaped to points of vantage. A low growl arose, for by then we could see that the objects were slaves.

They were alive! Heads and arms broke the surface of the sea. Even as we watched, one disappeared, then another, until finally all were gone, and the lowering clouds hid the slaver from our sight again.

The crew stirred and went about their duties.

The mate glanced at me. "Fair turns ye stomach, don't it? She'll beat us into Charles Town. We'll see her again."

"Why?" I demanded. "Why did they throw them overboard? They were alive!"

"Oh, indeedy? Ye saw that, too?"

"Yes! And so did the captain and most of the crew!"

"And as many of the passengers as was curious as ye, young sir!"

He was greatly amused by my horror-stricken countenance.

"Ye ain't seen much of the world, have ye, young feller?" he inquired.

"No—only Scotland."

"Ah, well, and in Scotland they don't have no call to throw slaves overboard! Well, I'll tell ye, sir. They throw the sick ones overboard because they'll be quarantined in Charles Town."

"What is wrong with quarantine?"

"Not a thing! Except nobody wants to buy sick slaves, and they'll be put back aboard the slaver. It's cheaper to heave 'em overboard than to feed 'em on the return trip to Afriky! That's why—cheaper!"

I was speechless. He grinned at me and went about his business. The mate was right—such knowledge did indeed turn one's stomach. I had no desire for food or for any companionship.

I went below and, bringing up my damp blanket, wrapped it about me. I crawled back among the ship's gear and settled myself for the night. No one would miss me in the crowded cabin. The other occupants would be glad of my room. I did not want to talk tonight.

The spanking of the sails was muffled. The clouds cleared. As I lay with my face to the now-darkening sky, I never felt more alone in my life.

A great homesickness for the hills and moors of Scotland came over me. I turned my face into my blanket and a muffled sound, halfway between a groan and a sob, escaped my lips, even though I was a great lad of seventeen.

There was a sudden movement, and a small figure

13

balanced on the coil of rope against which I lay. "Whist!" came a small whisper. "Be ye ailing, sir?"

"Nay," I denied it hotly, sitting up the better to make out the intruder. "I'm only clearing my throat. Who are you?"

"I'm Jamie McDowell of Edinburgh," came back the whisper.

I laughed. "Come closer, Jamie McDowell of Edinburgh. 'Tis impossible to get away from a Scotsman, even though one travels around the world!"

A cricket of a boy jumped from his perch and settled himself on a corner of my blanket. A thin face peered closer.

"And who are ye, my mon?" he asked, not abashed for all his small stature.

"Angus Ferguson, late of Glasgow," said I, not to be outdone in dignity.

"Eh!" he said, as grown-up as an old man. "And what is Master Ferguson a'doing aboard *The Wanderer?*"

"Going to seek my fortune in the Carolinas, but at present heartily wishing myself back at home," said I. "I take it that you also are seeking fame and fortune?"

"Ah, no," said the little fellow, instantly abandoning his role. "I've no such ambition. To tell you the truth, Angus, there wasn't food enough for all of us at home. I'm bound for my passage, and I hope to get a kind master to redeem the great expense the captain's been put to."

I was silent. There was never any lack of food in our home, even if a parsonage was not counted as a wealthy place.

"You're a wee bit of a lad," I said, "to be bound at such a tender age."

"I'm all of ten, sir," was the proud answer. "'Tis old enough to make a man's way in the world."

"Well, my friend Jamie," said I. "Fetch your blanket and we'll bed down together, seeing we are somewhat in the same case."

"I've only the clothes I stand up in," came the rejoinder.

"What!" I said. "The winds are a bit brisk for doing without a plaid."

"Only occasionally, and then I get up and run about to warm me."

"And you've slept on deck every night?" I inquired incredulously.

"Oh, yes, Angus. 'Tis the only way to stay healthy. Down below the air's so bad I have only to catch a whiff of it to wish myself above deck."

"Well, well," I said. "Settle down and share my blanket as a mattress, since you're like the birds and need only feathers."

Jamie sighed and settled down, curling himself about like a puppy. "'Tis very comfortable, Angus," he remarked sleepily.

I yawned and stretched wearily. But Jamie was restless and twisted and turned.

"Are ye asleep, Angus?"

"Nay."

"'Tis glad I am to have found ye, Angus. I kept looking for a friend but . . ."

"But what?"

"But no one offered."

I was ashamed. I remembered seeing the child in the weeks past, but he had been silent, dodging about on his own business. I put my hand on his thin shoulder and covered the small body against the salt spray.

"Go to sleep, little man," I admonished.

"Angus!" The whisper was urgent.

"Yes?"

"Did you see the West Indiaman?"

"Aye, that I did!"

"And . . . the things thrown overboard?"

"Aye."

"Were they truly people?" he asked.

"Aye, slaves."

Then came a question that brought me bolt upright. "Do ye think that God saw it, Angus?"

I swallowed and thought long before I answered. "Aye," I said. "He saw it."

"How can ye be so sure, Angus?"

"My father was a parson, and he knew the Good Book word for word. He said no sparrow falls but God knows of it."

"Then why didn't lightning fall from heaven on them that did the wicked deed?"

I gave him the only answer that came to me. "In his own good time, Jamie. Now sleep, child."

I lay awake long after Jamie slept. I thought of the deep faith of my dear, departed father. He would not doubt the judgment of the Lord, but I was not so sure. Miles of trackless ocean stretched between me and the certainties of home, and I, like Jamie, was afeard. It was best to sleep, and so I did, soothed by the ship's motion.

2
Charles Town

On this, our last day aboard *The Wanderer,* the sun shone bright and the waves danced. An air of excitement was about. The crew put the ship in order for our arrival. The passengers sat expectant, facing toward our destination, as if to catch sight of land the sooner. Every breeze brought us hints and odors of land, strange smells and fragrances of unseen vegetation. Birds circled the ship and flew away again. Then we discerned the low-lying islands of the Carolina coast and knew we were approaching our destination—the New World!

The New World. What a brave sound it had, and what visions it conjured up in my imagination of unknown, fantastic, and altogether satisfying adventures! From the time I was a boy, even younger than Jamie, I had become aware of the hold upon the minds of the people about me that any mention of the New World held.

I was but a wee lad when the clans of Scotland had been routed before the armies of the English. Though my sainted father was not a man to mourn the lost cause of the Stuarts, still he was sad and troubled about the plight of our country. He felt that for his only child the chances of life in a new world were brighter than a looking back to the glories of the old one. So when my dear mother died, he set about quietly to follow her, often telling me that when he was gone I was to spend my small inheritance to purchase passage to the colonies.

And so I did, being now an orphan. The clothes upon my back, a pound and a few shillings in my pocket, the

17

Good Book, and a fresh shirt in my seabag were my only possessions.

I doubted not that a good education—or such as passed for one in my father's parish—should help me on my way to fortune. I could read both Greek and Latin, had a knowledge of the mathematics, and could write a fair hand. I had heard that many less well-equipped than I had made their way in the colonies, and I counted on doing likewise.

Jamie was wild with excitement. He flew about from one vantage point to another, getting in the way of sailors and passengers alike. He hardly slept that night, nor did I, truth to tell.

Early light brought us into Charles Town harbor. We came slowly and carefully in, surrounded by numerous small craft, their sails spanking in the breeze. A low rampart of buildings lay in front of us, defined at either end by a cannon mounted on breastworks with the English flag flying above. Birds wheeled and darted in the sunshine, and large trees raised their heads inland.

"'Tis nothing like Edinburgh," said Jamie. "Where are the wild Indians?"

It was not the Indians we saw first, but black men hauling and pulling on the ropes that warped our ship into the dock. Loud, cheerful greetings passed between these men and the crew, gleeful at the prospect of hours of freedom ashore.

As I prepared to step upon the wharf, Jamie clutched my hand.

"Ye will not forget me, Angus?" he pleaded. "I cannot go ashore until someone buys my passage. The captain fears the redemptioners will run away."

"I'll not forget you, Jamie," I promised.

"And will ye tell a gentleman as wants to buy my time that I'll make him a good workman?"

"Aye, that I will, Jamie!"

"And, oh, Angus, I know it's a great favor to be asking, and me a bound boy, but do ye suppose the gentleman would let me learn me letters?"

Such an eagerness was in his voice and such a power of pleading in the upturned face, that my conscience smote me for being so eager to be off on my own business.

I dropped on my knees before him and grasped his shoulders—how thin they were!—and looked him in the eye.

"Jamie, my friend," I promised, "I'll find you a gentleman buyer, and the first article of the contract shall be that you'll get some schooling—one way or the other!"

"Oh, Angus! Thank ye, mon!" The smile on the small face was brilliant as the sunshine, as if the promise were already fulfilled.

So I went ashore bearing myself as confidently as if I could do all I had promised, but with a great doubt gnawing at my heart.

The city of Charles Town was like no other city that I had seen—not that my experience of cities was great. The warehouses and wharves swarmed with people—black men unloading the stores the ships brought, fishermen hawking their day's catch, and well-dressed merchants attired in the latest London fashions.

Conspicuous among the crowds were men and women balancing large, flat baskets expertly on their heads. They cried their wares in a melodious chant that was unintelligible to me.

Wandering about in the growing heat of the August day, I took to the shadows of the trees. My heavy wool jacket was too uncomfortable, so off it came to be stored in the seabag slung over my shoulder.

Everything conspired to delight the senses—the sea smells from the harbor behind me, the fragrance on every breeze, the bright clothing and gay chatter of the inhabitants.

The city was larger than I had thought. Near the busy customhouse was a small stone armory, guarded by smart-looking soldiers. Brick barracks were not far away, with more soldiers drilling there. I passed a large church under construction, its spire and columns rising above the surrounding trees.

Rows of neat wooden houses appeared, with shops interspersed among them, all painted in gay colors with flowers blooming in tiny dooryards. An occasional handsome house would rise two stories above the street, its double verandas oriented to catch the prevailing breezes.

The New World—or, at least, the corner of it called Charles Town—was inexpressibly delightful, and I could not imagine a pleasanter place in which to seek my fortune.

My wandering steps now turned back toward the harbor through the wide, sunny streets. Idly, I noticed a crowd of people curiously intent. As I came nearer I heard loud calls, or rather chants, in an odd singsong. Pushing through the men surrounding this activity, I found myself standing before a small open space. Here, huddled in various stages of terror and exhaustion, were exhibited black men, women, and even children. This was the slave market. It was to this place that the cargo of *The Indian Queen* had been destined.

I must have been conspicuous, staring with my mouth

open. I had heard such scenes described, but now I saw before me a slave auction.

A gentleman, whom I took to be an official, approached me.

"Young man," he inquired courteously, "are you here to buy?"

"No, sir," I said emphatically.

"This is not for public entertainment, so if you have no interest here, I must advise you to move on."

I turned my stunned attention from the slaves to my interrogator. He was a thin, sallow man, immaculately dressed in a dark suit and hat, his linen snowy and crisp.

"Are these the slaves from *The Indian Queen?*" I demanded.

A few bystanders turned curiously to observe us.

"No, my lad. *The Indian Queen's* cargo is still in quarantine and will be until it is ascertained that the slaves are healthy."

"What is left of them!"

My voice was raised and shaking with anger. More bystanders, now bored by the auction, surrounded us, apparently deciding that more entertainment was offered here.

The thin man surveyed me with a level gaze.

"What do you imply?"

"The Indian Queen dumped some of her cargo two days ago at sea. I was told that they were sick—slaves too sick to be accepted on shore."

"How do you know this?" The voice was icy.

"I saw them flung overboard."

"And where were you?"

"Aboard *The Wanderer,*" I replied.

The gentleman drew himself up to his full height. I was almost as tall as he. We must have made an odd contrast—the elegant gentleman in his dark clothes and I, red haired and angry, my clothes rumpled and stained from weeks aboard ship. Spectators gathered about us. They were quiet, apparently in deference to my questioner.

"This is a serious charge," he said.

"I am aware of it!" I answered, not to be intimidated.

The gentleman brought his hand up to his mouth and stared at me in silence. When he spoke again his voice was kinder.

"Let me introduce myself. I am Jarrell DuPree, a physician of Charles Town and an examiner for the City Board of Quarantine."

I took off my hat and made a bow, not to be outdone in courtesy.

"Angus Ferguson, late of Glasgow, at your service, sir!"

The keen eyes swept me from head to foot.

"Mr. Ferguson, you are somewhat young to make such a charge."

"I am seventeen years of age, sir," I protested.

I imagined I saw a sudden sadness in his face.

"Ah, yes, seventeen! I trust you will have someone to vouch for your veracity?"

"No, sir—only my word as a gentleman."

"But no witnesses who also saw the event you describe?"

"Oh, yes, sir! There were many who saw it—some of the crew of *The Wanderer* and as many of the passengers who were on deck at the time."

"It seems to me that we should first take this matter up with the owner of *The Indian Queen*. Will you accompany me to meet this gentleman?"

I looked about me. The spectators had been hanging

on every word of our conversation. They glared at me, and a mutter of disbelief ran about the small crowd surrounding us. It came to me that I was a disreputable figure, and why should anyone believe me?

My throat was dry, and my voice sounded hollow in my own ears. "Yes, sir," I answered.

"Very well," said the physician.

Turning we proceeded in silence down the street. Dr. DuPree walked beside me, but said no more until we approached the harbor.

"The warehouse and offices of the West India Trading Company are just ahead," he informed me.

We mounted a small flight of steps and came to a wooden platform. Before us was a large barnlike structure. Dr. DuPree summoned a boy from within and requested him to find the owner. Presently an erect figure of a man approached us; he, like my guide, was fashionably dressed.

"Ah, doctor!" he greeted the physician.

"Mr. Heyward, this lad is Mr. Angus Ferguson, come from Glasgow, and he has something to say to you"—glancing about at a few loiterers—"privately."

Mr. Heyward looked me over and then led the way within the cool, echoing shadows of the warehouse. He ushered us into a small cubicle.

"Be seated, gentlemen," offered our host. I shook my head, preferring to stand. It would be easier, I thought, clutching my hat nervously.

"I can see by your faces that the matter is of some importance," said Mr. Heyward.

"Yes," agreed Dr. DuPree. "It is important to me, in my position as examiner, and to you, John, as the owner of *The Indian Queen*. It is also of importance to our young friend here."

Mr. Heyward turned a puzzled face to me. "It has something to do with *The Indian Queen?*"

"Yes, sir. Two days ago I saw—we saw—*The Indian Queen* throw overboard a number of slaves."

Mr. Heyward shook his head. "Unfortunately, there are occasional deaths on crossing and the slaves must be buried at sea. Regrettable."

"But these were alive, sir!" I protested. "I saw them swimming—as many as a dozen, perhaps. Then they disappeared—just disappeared—one by one! The mate said slavers often did that to sick slaves who would not be accepted. He said it was cheaper than to feed them on the trip back to Africa!"

Mr. Heyward rose to his feet. "By God! Do you realize the seriousness of your charge?"

I couldn't answer. Dr. DuPree answered for me, "He does, John!"

Mr. Heyward glared at me.

"Are we to take it that you, alone, saw this?"

I had got my voice back again. "Oh, no, sir! The crew and passengers on the deck of *The Wanderer* saw it too."

He sat down heavily. Both men looked at each other without speaking. Mr. Heyward shook his head. "I should have got out of this Guinea business long ago, Jarrell! I shall do so yet!"

"But this affair has to be disposed of immediately," reminded Dr. DuPree.

"Yes, yes," agreed Mr. Heyward. He sat in deep thought. "Perhaps this will be the way to come at the truth. The captain and mate of *The Queen* will be here shortly to render a tally of the cargo. I'll confront them with your statement, my lad. It will be wiser if you are not here. H'm! Jarrell, please take him to *The Wanderer* and

24

get that captain's statement. Wait until you see that I'm alone and then return."

"One question, lad," called Mr. Heyward as Dr. DuPree and I walked to the door. "You said this happened two days ago?"

"Yes, sir, at sunset. We were running between thundershowers. Perhaps they thought we could not see them."

He nodded. Out in the sunshine again, we made our way to where *The Wanderer* was docked. Dr. DuPree hailed the ship, and the captain came to stand above us on the deck.

"Jarrell DuPree, examiner for the City Board of Quarantine. May I come aboard, captain?"

"Aye, sir, ye're welcome."

We walked up the gangplank to confront the captain. "I would like some information that you are in a position to give me," Dr. DuPree said.

The captain eyed me suspiciously, "Aye, sir, if I can."

"I'm sure you can help me, sir. This young man—Mr. Angus Ferguson, lately one of your passengers—says that many on deck saw slaves thrown overboard from *The Indian Queen* two days ago. I think it was at sunset. Did you see any such happening?"

A great silence descended. The busy crew gradually stopped all activity. The captain peered at me closely, as if he had never seen me before.

"He says that, does he?" he mused.

"He does," said Dr. DuPree.

"Well, now," said the captain regretfully. "Ain't it odd, sir, but I didn't see no such thing."

I was startled. "Oh, sir, you did indeed! Most of the crew on deck and some of the passengers saw it too! The slaves were alive, for some of them stayed on top of the waves, and I could see them swimming for a little while."

The captain shook his head sadly. He turned to the attentive crew and raised his voice. "This here lad says he seen slaves cast off *The Indian Queen* two days ago. I didn't see no such thing, but then 'twas nearly dark about sunset. Did any of you see such a happening, eh, mates?"

No one spoke. No one moved. The captain turned to Dr. DuPree and shook his head. "You see how it was, sir. We was all busy with the ship at that time, like always. This boy's probably touched in the head, and who'd think it to look at him?"

And then a small voice spoke above our heads; but if it had been thunder, it could not have had more effect. "I saw them cast overboard, sir!"

There, hanging from his usual perch, was Jamie.

"And they were swimming, sir, just as Angus said," Jamie assured the doctor.

"What's your name, boy?" called the doctor.

"Jamie McDowell, sir, of Edinburgh."

Dr. DuPree glanced about. His lips curled in distaste. "Remarkable!" he commented. "Only two Scotsmen had sharp enough eyes to see something that escaped everyone else!"

He turned abruptly. "We won't take more of your time, captain!"

Motioning me to follow, he strode angrily down the gangplank. I followed and on the wharf turned and looked back. Jamie had not moved. All eyes were on him.

"Wait, Dr. DuPree," I begged. "Look!"

Dr. DuPree turned and took in Jamie's situation at a glance. Fear seized me.

"The captain will take his spite out on Jamie! The boy's a redemptioner and can't leave the ship until his passage is paid."

Then a hope sprang in me. "Would you buy his passage, sir? I'll be responsible. I'll pay you as soon as I can! I can't leave him!"

"Captain!" called out the doctor.

"Aye, sir?"

"I'll buy young Jamie's passage."

"Will ye, now, sir? That's kind of ye!"

"How much?"

"It'll be £10. A boy like that eats a lot."

"Send him down!"

"Now?"

"Immediately!"

There was a sudden movement, and Jamie came flying down the gangplank.

"I'll send the money tomorrow," said the doctor, and we three walked quickly away from the ship. I hoped fervently that was the last I ever saw of *The Wanderer*.

Jamie's hand stole into mine as we marched away. "I knew ye'd come for me, Angus! I wasn't afeard . . . much, that is!" he concluded.

I laughed. He was an odd contradiction of a boy! I swung his small body up to my shoulder, where he sat perched like a sparrow as we followed the good doctor along the wharf.

We arrived at Mr. Heyward's office sooner than we anticipated. The door opened, and two men swaggered out looking so villainous they could only be the officers of *The Indian Queen*. They made elaborate bows to the doctor, but gave me hard stares as they passed. I caught a glimpse of a gold ring in the ear of the smaller man.

27

The Red Wind

Mr. Heyward looked up in surprise as we entered. His curious gaze took in the smiling Jamie.

"Master Jamie McDowell of Edinburgh, John!" said Dr. DuPree. "The only man on *The Wanderer*. He spoke up to testify to young Ferguson's veracity. No one else said a word."

Mr. Heyward smiled sourly.

"Well, my men swore by all that's holy that they threw overboard only dead bodies." He looked at me. "I'm afraid no one but ourselves will believe your story, young man. And there's an end to it."

I turned my hat around in my hands. There was nothing to say—and yet there was, too!

"I'm sorry, sir, for making all the trouble for you. I thought"— surely, I wasn't going to show my disappointment to the two gentlemen standing silent—"I thought it was the thing my father would have wanted me to do."

There was one last thing to do before I left the gentlemen.

"Dr. DuPree, I have only a little money left, but when I find some employment, I'll repay the money you laid out for Jamie. I'm much more in your debt for trusting me."

Dr. DuPree smiled, "Don't worry about Jamie, lad. My daughter will enjoy having someone around to feed and clothe"— he seemed to be having trouble with his voice, but it came out strongly—"and so will I!"

"Well, then, good day, gentlemen," I said, and walked out into the bright sunshine.

I heard feet flying down the platform behind me, and Jamie flung himself upon me and clung to my knees.

"Oh, Angus, Angus!" he wept. "Do not forget me!"

"No, no, Jamie, indeed I won't! There, now." I knelt and attempted to wipe away the tears from the woeful face. "There, now! I'll come to see how you are getting on"—I glanced at Dr. DuPree for his permission, which was given by a nod—"and besides, as soon as I can I'll buy your time from the good doctor. Remember, you said you are old enough to make a man's way in the world!"

"Did I say that?"

"Indeed you did!"

"Well," said Jamie, taking a deep breath, "goodbye, Angus."

And so I parted from my friend who cast many a backward glance at me as he followed Dr. DuPree.

3
The Bookshop
and the Barracks

The sun was growing hotter. I had been in and out of shops and offices on a long tour, and everywhere the answer was the same. There was no opening, not even an hour's work for a stranger. Disconsolate, I turned aimlessly and began to retrace my steps. I recognized the small bookshop where I had earlier inquired for work. The owner, standing in the doorway, called to me.

"How is it going, my lad?"

"I cannot find employment anywhere, sir."

He looked me over.

"Hungry, no doubt?"

I flushed even redder than I was.

"I am not yet reduced to begging, sir."

He smiled. "No offense, my lad. However, you might come within and share some bread and cheese with me."

I did not wait for a second invitation. It being the dinner hour for the citizens of Charles Town, the shop was deserted. We sat at a window and looked out upon the street so that no customer might be lacking a welcome from the owner.

The bread and cheese were speedily eaten, washed down with great cups of tea. I began to feel hope rise once more.

The owner had courteously waited until I finished the last crumb.

"I take it that you are a newcomer, lad."

"Yes, sir. I'm just off *The Wanderer*. Angus Ferguson of Glasgow at your service."

"Aye, I recognized the country of your origin when first you spoke. I'm a Scotsman myself—John Duncan—a Lowlander, you'll understand. I take you for a Highlander."

"Yes, sir." I surveyed my host with interest. He was small but quick and lithe upon his feet.

"You'll find many of our country here in the Carolinas. Why we Scots should hanker for a low country like this coast with no mountains and no heather, I can't imagine."

"Perhaps it's the sea," I hazarded a guess.

"Aye, perhaps." He glanced at my weatherbeaten clothes. "And you'll be wishing to make your way among us?"

"Yes, sir. I had no mind to be a country parson like my father, and I decided to see the world."

"Aye, the world!" he mused. "'Twas once upon a time my own ambition, also. But as you can see, I've settled upon a wee corner of it here. 'Tis none so bad—a tiny bookshop. There's a many in the colonies that take to the printed word and perhaps are more avid for it, since 'tis with some difficulty it is come by."

I thought of the many books that had once surrounded me in my father's study and recollected that I had grown tired of them and had longed to see the world outside. I sighed and resolved to tell my troubles to this kind stranger.

"Mr. Duncan, 'tis desperate I am. I hoped to see this part of the world, but never gave much thought to how I should fare in it."

"Aye," he agreed, "when one is sixteen . . . "

"Seventeen, sir," I said, drawing myself up a bit taller.

"Even seventeen," he said, smiling slightly, "ye give no thought of the morrow, as it says in the Good Book.

31

'Tis only human. The world is rosy, and there's never such a thing as being hungry or thirsty."

"Yes, sir," I confessed, shamefaced. "I see I was overhasty to come without some arrangement . . . "

"Ah, no, lad," he said heartily. "Carefulness will come. But you should know you've come at a very upsetting time in the colonies, and we've all been a bit preoccupied. Perhaps that is why you've not got too warm a reception."

"Why, what's afoot, sir?"

"The French—surely even hidden in the Highlands you've heard about the Frenchmen's war!" he demanded.

"Yes, of course." I recollected tales of marches and battles, and it came to me that in these very colonies a famous general had met his death.

"You have had your nose in the books!" my host remarked. He drew a long line in the dust of the shelf before us. "See here—that long line is the Mississippi—"

"What a strange name!"

"Remember it, my lad. That river runs north and south. About the bottom of it are three French settlements—New Orleans, Mobile, and Natchez. Then at the top around the Great Lakes, and farther to the northeast in Canada, there are more French forts than you can shake a stick at! Every one bristling with Frenchies—and they mean to stay there!"

"But, sir," I said in my wisdom, "Canada is a thousand miles away. Surely 'tis no danger to His Majesty's colonies."

For answer he drew a line halfway down the Mississippi, angling to the northeast.

"But, see, here is the River Ohio, *La Belle Rivière,* and

believe me, 'tis a French river along which an Englishman goes at his peril.''

Then he drew a line to the right paralleling the original line. "Now here is the sea coast from New England to Georgia. Our people are confined by the ocean on the east and by the mountains to the north and west. North of us are the French and south of us, the Spanish.''

I stared at the lines in the dust. I had thought the colonies so secure to the Crown that I had not given the matter a second thought.

"Now, look," said Mr. Duncan, as he laid a broad hand between the Mississippi and the mountains. "Here lies a great valley from the Gulf of Mexico to the Great Lakes. This is the richest land in the world—forests, prairies, rivers—with game beyond counting. Who stands here between the French and us?''

I knew the answer. "The Indians!''

"Aye, the fiercest warriors in the world!''

Mr. Duncan took his hand from over the map and looked at it a long time.

"The French have won so far. Most of the Indians are their allies. One nation is our friend.''

He put his finger on an area west of Charles Town. "That nation is the Cherokee. They are loyal today because we provide better and cheaper trade goods than the French. Tomorrow, who can tell? Four years ago our royal governor, at their request, built a fort among them. 'Tis over the mountains, among the Overhill Cherokee, as they are called.''

I remembered a tale often told me as a child. "My father said when he was a young lad seven Cherokee chiefs came to London.''

"That was thirty years ago.''

"He saw them then. He told me of the proud bearing

33

of the chiefs and of how King George received them at the court."

"One of the seven still lives and can be seen occasionally on a visit to the governor here."

"Here!" I could not imagine an Indian chieftain striding down the streets of Charles Town.

"He's a famous chief of the Cherokees. His name is Attakullakulla, and we call him the Little Carpenter. He is their peace chief. I suppose you would call him their prime minister. The governor consults him about as frequently as he consults any Indian chief—which is not often!"

"Why should the royal governor consult an Indian chief, Mr. Duncan?"

Mr. Duncan looked at me over his glasses in pity of my ignorance. "My boy, don't you recollect what happened to a big fine army led by General Braddock four years ago?"

"Sir, I was a mere lad of thirteen four years ago—more concerned with running over the moors than with bothering my head with what happened to English generals."

"Well, the famous general, like our Governor Lyttelton here, paid no attention to the Indians either. He lost an army and his life for neglecting them! My advice to you, my lad, is never to tangle with an Indian—much less a Cherokee!"

I smiled. "I assure you, Mr. Duncan, I have no intention of tangling with a Cherokee or with any other aborigine!"

My lofty tone amused Mr. Duncan, no doubt, for he cautioned, "You have much to learn in this new world, my lad!"

We parted friends, however, and he reminded me to call on him for assistance, if needed.

The more I thought of Mr. Duncan's map of the colonies, the more it seemed to me to be a fine thing to fight the Frenchmen. The life of a soldier surely would be more exciting than that of a merchant or a scrivener, which up until then I had considered my lot in life. In the free air of the colonies, one could be anything one desired! I drew myself up taller and wondered how a red coat and a sword would become me. I turned my steps toward the sound of the drums and was soon admiring the drilling going on in the square fronting the barracks. The variously garbed recruits were being put through the drill by a noisy sergeant who seemed to be mightily displeased with the ragged lines. Surely I could do no worse. Indeed, now that I thought about it, I was certain that I should make His Majesty a most useful soldier.

I approached the door to the barracks through which came and went a number of hurrying soldiers. Two magnificent uniformed figures guarded the door. Screwing up my courage, I took off my hat and stood tongue-tied before them.

One swiveled his eyes at me, not moving so much as one inch his erect posture.

"Move on, boy!" he growled, "No loitering 'ere!"

"But, sir, I should like to enlist."

He stared at me in utter amazement. "Me sainted mother!" he said with upraised eyes. He appealed to the soldier across the doorway. "D'ye hear that, corporal? Now we've got babes as wants to wear the king's uniform!"

The corporal brought his eyes to bear upon me. "Does 'e, now?" he inquired softly.

"Aye, 'e does, corporal!"

"Ah!" said the corporal. "Can ye fire a musket, young sir?"

"No, sir."

"Can ye squads right and about-face?"

"No, sir."

"Can ye double and go in with the bayonet?"

"Of course not! I haven't been trained to do so!"

No doubt, I was as red as my hair with vexation. Surely it would be a much easier thing to face enemy shells than the scorn of these extremely tall men.

"What *can* ye do then, laddie?" growled the first soldier.

"I can cypher and write a fair hand!" I said belligerently.

"Now, now, corporal! We're reduced to fightin' the French with goose quills and ink!"

He turned his attention full on me and gave me a fierce glare.

"Go back to school, laddie, and leave firing cannon and handling ropes to your betters. And don't bother Captain Stuart—'e's got more to do just now than recruiting such undesirables!"

Regretting any thoughts of a military career, I clapped my hat upon my head and strode angrily away, followed by the laughter of my tormentors.

4
Pursued

Many hot, dusty hours later, I sat alone on the wharf. The sun was going down on my first day in the New World, and I was hungry.

Everywhere the answer was the same: nothing! Strangely, everyone seemed to know what events had occurred earlier in the day, because the first response to my inquiry about employment was always the question, "Are you the boy from *The Wanderer?*"

I could not decide whether my part in reporting the events aboard *The Indian Queen* was considered commendable or threatening. No matter what people's opinions of my actions were, the result was still the same—I had no means in all the city to make myself an honest living!

As I sat watching the restless waves of the harbor in the fading light, I was forced to admit an unpleasant fact—I did not have the proper skills to make my way in the New World.

I did not know how to fire a gun, nor yet a cannon, as the sentries at the barrack's door had so contemptuously informed me. My Latin and Greek were of no use since the merchants and traders of the town wanted someone who was versed in the Indian languages.

Of course, it was possible to appeal to Dr. DuPree or to Mr. Heyward for help. Nevertheless, I was determined to avoid this if possible. I was already in Dr. DuPree's debt; his assuming the responsibility for Jamie took a great load off my mind.

I had bought a loaf of bread while passing a bakery, so now I took it out of my seabag, arranged myself comfortably with my back against a corner of the warehouse, hung my heels off the wharf, and began my solitary supper.

A deep voice spoke above me. "Ain't permitted to lollygag around de warehouse!"

Startled, I looked up to see the biggest, blackest man I had ever seen. He wore workmen's clothes and ragged shoes. His face was impassive. I swallowed the bite of bread and could not speak.

He spoke again, "De patrol'll get you here. Ain't a safe place, nohow. Too many sailorman about."

I scrambled to my feet. "I have no place to go."

He stooped to look more closely at me. "Ain't you de boy who spoke to Marse Heyward 'bout *De Indian Queen?*"

"Yes."

He grinned. "You brave fella!"

"It was the truth!"

"Heh! Truth get you in heap o' trouble! Come home wif me, boy!"

I was taken by surprise. "I can't pay you."

He spoke fiercely. "Ain't said nothin 'bout pay!"

He turned, and I gathered up my belongings and followed obediently. He burst into song, and we marched along the darkening streets to the beat of the song's rhythm.

We came presently to a small dilapidated house, leaning for support against the side of a large building. A tiny black woman, neatly dressed, rose from the small porch to greet us.

"Tina," called my host, "got enough in de pot for two hungry fella?"

Tina laughed in answer and hurried inside where delicious smells came from a pot hanging over the fire on the hearth.

And so I was made welcome in the bare, spotless house of Abram, "Marse Benn's man," as he introduced himself.

The contents of the pot was a savory stew, accompanied by crisp bread baked on the clean-swept hearth. I was told that it was called a pone. It occasioned great laughter that I did not know that a pone was made of the meal of Indian corn.

Abram proceeded to instruct me in other matters as we sat on the small porch while Tina busied herself inside. A cool night breeze was blowing from the harbor.

"Boy," warned Abram, "you make big trouble for de cap'n of *De Indian Queen*—heap o' trouble. He ain't happy 'bout it one little bit! Slaves big business, boy. You marked man!"

"Abram," I asked, "do you suppose that was why I couldn't get a job today?"

"Mebbe so, mebbe not. It don't make no nevermind."

He sat quiet crooning to himself. Finally he came to a conclusion.

"Heh! Mebbe you lift bales alongside of me?"

"Oh, yes, Abram. I'll do anything!"

"Hard work—hot work! You is light for such, but we try!"

He called within, "Tina, borry some work clothes from yo' cousin for boy, here. He work alongside of me tomorrow."

Tina hurried off, and Abram explained the job ahead of us tomorrow.

"Marse Benn, he contract me to Marse Elliot—he de packtrain boss. Cap'n Stuart, he buildin' a fire under

39

Marse Elliot to get onto de tradin' path to de Overhill fort. Marse Elliot, he be glad to see you—even if you is a white boy."

I was lost in all this explanation, but trusted that Abram knew whereof he spoke. Presently Tina returned with clean-smelling work clothes. Abram found a blanket and arranged it as a mattress for me on the porch.

"Sleep here tonight. We find you place tomorrow."

So, well fed and welcomed in the New World, and with a job awaiting me on the morrow, I fell asleep.

Thus, I returned to *The Wanderer* as a dockhand. In my workman's clothes and the hat Abram found for me I was not recognized I was sure. Few of the crew were about, and those who were had their minds ashore.

Abram was right. Working at the wharves was hard work—and hot work! The sun beat down mercilessly. I was glad indeed to have the cotton work clothes that Tina provided instead of my heavy wool garments.

The cargo aboard ship was in barrels and tightly sewn bales. They were brought up from the ship's hold, then lifted by rope and pulley from the deck to the wharf. There the containers were broken open, and the contents arranged in seeming confusion for the merchants and individual buyers to claim.

The scene was a madhouse it seemed to me—men heaving on the tackles and crying out to passersby to beware, merchants seeking their own wares, and bystanders wandering aimlessly to observe all the excitement.

Mr. Elliot, Abram's employer, was in charge of a section of the wharf where supplies for his packtrain were gathered. A thin, sour-visaged man, he stayed busy running between ship and stockpile, keeping a record of the unloading.

After an hour in the hot sun I felt that I was an old hand

at the job. Although my muscles were unaccustomed to such unusual exertion, the excitement of these new surroundings kept me from feeling fatigue. I stood up and, with my back to the busy crowd, watched a barrel high over my head being lowered from the deck of the ship. Suddenly I felt a violent blow, and I was flung headfirst into the narrow space between the ship and the wharf.

Surprise took my breath away, and I went under the murky waters that closed above me. I fought my way to the air and sunlight. The wooden hull of the ship on one side and the great stones of the wharf on the other towered above me. The little waves slapped and hissed.

Abram's shout of alarm came from a distance. "Boy, boy! Where are you?"

I yelled in answer and saw his astonished face peering down. He called encouragement and within minutes flung down a rope. I was hoisted to the wharf, dripping. "Someone shoved me!" I said when I could get my breath.

"Who, boy?" he demanded.

We turned and searched the crowd carefully, but no face was turned to observe us. I looked down into the narrow space from which I had been lifted. I shivered.

Abram drew me back from the ship's side and the dark waters that lapped at the wharf. "Back up to something, boy," he commanded. "If they come at you den, they have to come in front."

He looked about again. "Somebody don't like you, for true!"

By the time the late afternoon sun slanted across the harbor, I was weary indeed. Abram, however, was tireless. His hearty laugh and cheerful voice rang out above all other noises. He was everywhere—instructing,

41

encouraging, placating, arguing—the major-domo of the wharf. He had assigned me to the deck of the ship where my duties were to keep straight the ropes that were engaged in lowering the bales to the wharf below.

A fresh breeze sprang up, and I straightened from my task, enjoying the coolness. While I stood idle for a moment, a horse and rider approached from the city. The horse was a mettlesome thing, young and wiry, but the rider had complete control. As they came nearer, I saw that the rider was a girl, sitting her mount easily, her long riding skirts billowing. She reined in the horse and seemed to be searching for someone. She raised her face to the deck, and I saw smooth dark hair and flashing eyes.

Seeing me standing there she called, "Where is Abram?"

I turned and beckoned to Abram. He approached and greeted her as an old friend.

"Here I be, Miss Vannie."

She called, "My seed order from England, Abram! Do you know where I can find it?"

"Missy, ask Marse Elliot. He know. He on de wharf."

"Thank you," called the rider as she turned her horse.

The stranger's voice and erect carriage intrigued me.

"Who is she, Abram?" I asked.

"Dr. DuPree's little gal. She one smart one!"

"How is that?"

"She de boss lady of his plantations. She smarter than her pappy's overseers."

Then I remembered that Dr. DuPree had said his daughter would be pleased to have Jamie in charge. It appeared that Jamie was in good hands indeed.

I watched her progress down the length of the wharf until she was lost to my sight.

As the shadows lengthened, workmen left the deck and wharf, and quiet descended. I was glad. The hot, tarry smell of the wharf was heavy in my nostrils, and I was tired, thirsty, and hungry.

Abram stayed until the last. When Mr. Elliot came by, we were instructed that tomorrow's task would be to arrange the loads for the packhorses.

"Be sure to be here early, Abram!"

"Yas, suh! Yas, suh!"

Mr. Elliot eyed me thoughtfully, "You worked very well today, lad."

"Thank you, sir." I gathered it was not an everyday occurrence to have a word of praise from the trader.

"I thought you weren't strong enough to make a good hand, but you kept up with Abram."

I had to be honest. "Abram helped me, Mr. Elliot."

"No doubt, no doubt," said Mr. Elliot testily as he left.

Abram turned a pleased face to me. "You satisfy de boss, boy. He don't want for to take you."

If Abram only knew how many times I had been tempted to give up in the hot sun!

Fetching my seabag, stored near a corner of the warehouse, I jumped down from the wharf and headed for the water's edge.

"Where you go, boy?" Abram called. "Tina got de kettle on."

"I'm going to take a swim to cool off, Abram. I know the way back."

A wary half-whisper came to me as he turned to go. "Be careful, boy!"

I stripped and swam lazily in the waters of the harbor, idly watching the light fade in the sky. I felt pleased with my progress in the New World. Certainly I had not anticipated working as a lowly dockhand, but the knowledge that I had done a good job was a source of pride. I had supper awaiting me and work to do on the morrow. What more could one ask?

Yet a nagging thought kept intruding: Who could have pushed me into the harbor? The unexpected blow was not an accident. I remembered Abram's way of putting it: "Somebody don't like you, for true!"

Refreshed, I came ashore and scrubbed my garments with sand, having no soap. I got into my heavy wool garments again. Carrying my clean, damp work clothes in a roll, I started out for Tina's hospitality, whistling happily.

The early night was loud with sounds. Insects shrilled and clamored from every bush, and unseen birds sang noisily from the treetops. I could hear far-off laughter and singing.

As I walked, it seemed that an echo of my own footsteps came back to my ears. When I stopped to determine if it were indeed so, the echoes stopped. Reassured, I walked on, but more quickly. Suddenly in the silence I clearly heard footsteps behind me. Uneasy, I turned and searched the shadows. Nothing moved. Above my head the birds were suddenly quiet.

Then, I heard the sound of running feet and Abram's urgent voice calling, "Boy! Boy!"

I answered and ran toward his hurrying figure. Without a word, he drew me into the shadow of a building and whispered in my ear, "Listen!"

We held our breaths. Nothing stirred. Then we heard a small sound—metal striking against metal.

Abram whispered, "For true, someone follow! Run to town, fast, away from de harbor. I run de other way and make lots of noise! Run!"

By this time I could see more clearly, and what I saw spurred me into action—men crouching in the shadows!

44

Pursued

I sped into the dark street, running silently, and for my life, I knew. Behind me I could hear Abram's yells as he, too, ran. I flung away my clothes and seabag, and ran as I had never run before.

As I fled down the wide, dark streets, faint lights shone in occasional windows giving me some indication of where I was. Ahead of me loomed the bulk of the church I had seen the day before. With a sobbing breath, I heaved myself onto the portico. Retreating against one of the huge columns, I scanned the way I had come. I heard a low whistle and the sound of running feet approaching. My pursuers had found my direction!

I jumped from my place of refuge and ran down the broad street, keeping close to houses and fences. I cared not whether I kept silent or no. Far away I heard a new sound—a horse's muffled cantering.

In the darkness, I stumbled and fell sprawling. A length of a picket fence had fallen across my path. I wrenched it away and thus had a cudgel of sorts at hand. My strength had given out. My breath came in gasps, but now I had a weapon.

I ran again. I found a large column supporting iron gates and resolved to make my stand here, mindful of Abram's admonition that thus if they came at me, they would have to come in front.

Crouching, I awaited my pursuers. Three men ran past, then stopped and listened. So many! My heart beat so loudly in my own ears that I felt sure it could be heard.

The low whistle came again, and a gesture from the first man turned the others about, and they came toward me. As they closed silently about me, I stood erect and yelled, "Abram! Abram!" and struck at one of my pursuers.

He went down, surprised, no doubt, but the other two

leaped for me. I struck again, but my wooden weapon was torn from my grasp, and I stood helpless.

My assailants were winded too, their breaths whistling in their throats. The one I had struck rose to his feet. The dull light gleamed on knives held by two of them. One brandished the picket. They paused. They were in no hurry.

"Now, you scum!" growled the man with the gold earring. "We'll learn ye to meddle in what's none of yer business!"

He raised his knife, and I yelled again. It seemed to me that the horse's canter had become a gallop. I kicked at the stomach of the man nearest me, and he fell to his knees just as the man with the picket brought it down on my head.

In that second, confusion broke out all around. I could hear Abram's shouts approaching. A horse and rider burst into the figures surrounding me, and I leaped for a stirrup to save myself from the rearing hooves above my head and hung on, frantic. Blood streamed into my eyes, blinding me.

I distinguished a new sound—a whip whistled in the air above my head, and my attackers, yelling, gave way and ran.

Then a soft voice spoke above me. "Are you hurt?"

I shook my head, released my clutch on the stirrup, and stepped back from my rescuer. My knees gave way, and, ignominiously, I sat down.

Abram knelt beside me and wiped the blood away from my eyes.

"Did they knife you, boy?" he asked. I shook my throbbing head. I had not breath enough to answer.

He stood up and laughed, "Missy, you come just in de nick of time!"

"I heard yelling, Abram, and thought they were after you."

"No, Missy. Boy here, he dé target."

"Is he hurt?"

"Little. Can't tell."

"Bring him to the house. Father will look after him."

Abram stooped and lifted me in his huge arms as if I had been a child. Trotting after my rescuer, he carried me swiftly down the dark streets.

When he stopped, I struggled to my feet determined to be as dignified as possible and walked up some steps. Abram kept his arm about my sagging shoulders as we waited in a wide, echoing hall. Lights and people approached. I recognized Dr. DuPree's clipped soft speech and then the even softer tones of his daughter's voice. Then, I tell it to my disgrace, I fainted.

5
The House on Meeting Street

It seemed to me I ran all night long, footsteps pounding behind me, ominous and promising nothing but disaster. I woke in darkness and for a moment thought I must be home in Scotland. But no. A strange bird was singing outside the open window—a bird I had never heard in Scotland.

The light came swiftly, and a fresh breeze stirred the curtains in the large room. Facing me was a fireplace, and above it hung a large portrait. Mirrors shone upon the walls. I lay in a soft, wide bed.

As I stirred and sat upright, my head began a savage pounding. Putting my hand up, I found it bandaged. I struggled to my feet and discovered my old friend Jamie—fully dressed and stretched across the threshold sound asleep. Such a changed fellow! His skin was as clean and pink as that of a new baby! As I stood above him, he stirred and his eyes opened. He sat up, instantly awake.

"Angus! I was sleeping here to keep the robbers out, if they should come again."

I laughed although it set my head to aching again.

"Jamie, my lad! They'll never come with you to protect me!"

"That was what I told Missy. She let me sleep here."

"Oh, yes, it was the good doctor who bandaged my head."

"Yes, and 'twas a hard time he and Abram had getting ye to bed, so sound asleep ye were."

48

I blushed to think of it and whispered urgently, "Where then are my clothes, Jamie?"

"Taken to be washed, Angus. There was blood all over them. But Dr. DuPree said for ye to wear these laid out here. He thought they might fit."

By this time we could hear the sounds of morning activity in the house. I struggled into the fine garments that Jamie pointed out to me. When I dressed, I looked into a mirror and hardly recognized myself, so vastly improved I was! Nevertheless, the soft shoes provided for me could not be managed, so Jamie went flying out the hall to find my own good leather ones.

A knock came at the door, and a thin black man bowed and inquired after my health.

"Dr. DuPree would like to see you, young sir, when you are awake."

I professed myself entirely awake and eager to meet the good doctor. As we were talking Jamie came back with my shoes, cleaned and shined as they had never been before. Thus properly attired I followed the servant. Jamie excused himself to his duties. He assured me he was very necessary in the running of the household.

Dr. DuPree's study was a small room opening off the veranda. It was fragrant with the smell of herbs and elixirs.

He rose to greet me, smiling.

"I see you are remarkably improved, young man! Good, good!"

"I fear I was a great burden last night, sir."

The doctor shrugged. "Since Mr. Heyward and I were partly to blame for your difficulties, it was only right that I should make amends."

"Your daughter was truly the heroine, Dr. DuPree. I

49

remember very little, except that she beat off the men until Abram arrived."

"Yes, so Abram informed me."

A quick step came at the door, and there she stood. I could understand Abram's and Jamie's devotion. Slender and erect, her thin face framed by dark hair, she was as beautiful as a thoroughbred.

A smile lighted her face. "I see your patient has almost recovered, Father!"

I bowed. "Thanks to your timely arrival, Mistress DuPree."

She turned to her father. "Now, sir, perhaps you will allow that my night gallops are to some purpose."

Dr. DuPree regarded his daughter fondly.

"My daughter insists on exercising the horse at night, thinking it cooler than the day."

"It is only honest to confess that I prefer to ride astride, sir, and do not wish to cause a scandal in the city."

Her father shook his head. "A most unmaidenly thing!"

"Our guest has not breakfasted, Father, and here we stand gossiping while he is no doubt fainting from hunger!"

My head had never ceased throbbing, and I was only too glad to follow the doctor to a seat on the shaded veranda. Two servants, preceded by a careful Jamie laden down with silver and china, arranged a table and set a fragrant bowl of broth before me.

"We breakfasted long ago," said Mistress DuPree. "Father thought that broth would be the very thing for his patient."

Indeed, it was delicious. Never had I been more carefully attended—the bread and broth were soon gone, and more was brought. For all the careful attention, I should cheerfully have had my head cracked again!

Dr. DuPree called for his hat and took his leave. He announced that he would inform his friend Mr. Heyward about the attack and would ascertain if more information could be had about the scoundrels who had set upon me.

After Mistress DuPree excused herself to be about her morning duties, I returned to the room where I had slept the night before.

There above the mantel was the large picture that had engaged my attention when I first awoke. It was a portrait of a lad of my own age. His figure was slim and elegant, his thin dark face, smiling. His face seemed curiously familiar, as if I had seen him fleetingly or had dreamed of him. An odd thought, indeed!

I reentered the wide echoing hall that traversed the house. Doors stood open at either end, and a cool breeze swept through. Following the sounds, I stepped onto a wide veranda.

Across the yard below me were several small buildings. Slaves—men, women, and children—were scurrying about from one building to another. In the middle of the quadrangle formed by the buildings was a roofed well. A black man pulled on a creaking windlass and brought a dripping bucket to the curb of the well. He poured the water into a nearby tub and started the bucket on its downward journey again.

As I came down the stairs all activity halted, and alert eyes watched me for all the world as fowl watch a hawk circling in the sky above. Sudden laughter broke out, and an old black woman called, "Missy, here be de po' boy set upon by thieves!"

Mistress DuPree appeared in the doorway of one of the larger structures. A spotless apron protected her dress.

51

"Mr. Ferguson!" she exclaimed. "Are you well enough to walk about?"

"Except for a headache, Mistress DuPree, I have recovered sufficiently so I need not be classified as an invalid. May I add that my name is Angus, to my friends."

She regarded me with laughter in her eyes. "And I am Savannah to my friends."

She untied her apron and handed the garment to a servant. She tucked an escaping lock of hair into its proper place and led the way to the welcome shade of the veranda.

"Do sit in the shade, sir. The sun must be too hot for your poor head. I am quite ready to stop for a bit."

She seated herself and, drawing a basket nearer, drew out of it a garment and began sewing, her face intent on the chore.

I sat regarding this half-child, half-woman—an enigma who rode astride at midnight and was the manager of a busy household, sober and laughing by turns. I had never seen anyone like her.

"Mistress . . ."

Her dark eyes were raised for a moment.

"Savannah," I continued. "I first saw you at the wharf when you inquired of Abram's whereabouts."

"Oh, yes! Were you the man above me on the ship's deck?"

"Yes. Abram had been kind enough to find me employment."

"My father told me of your accusation of the slaver's captain."

"It all came to nothing," I said bitterly.

Her needle paused for a moment.

"Then, no doubt, you regret your involvement?"

"No, indeed!" I blurted. "I should do it again!"

"Even at the expense of a broken head?"

I was goaded beyond bearing. "Now you are laughing at me!"

The sewing that had previously so engrossed her attention was put down, and a smiling face was raised to regard me.

"I confess that I was indulging in levity, sir—a habit that my father much deplores in females! I have often heard that a Scotsman is hard put to it to change his opinions, and now I believe it. Pray forgive me!"

I, too, laughed. "I forgive you for anything! I do not forget that you came to my rescue last night. Nevertheless, I must say that my Scottish pride is in the dust. To be rescued by a girl . . ." I hesitated for a word.

"Is exceedingly galling, is it not?"

"It is indeed!"

"Perhaps I like you all the better for your Scottish pride being somewhat diminished!"

At noon we sat down in the cool, high-ceilinged dining room to a welcome meal. Dr. DuPree sat at the head of the table, Savannah at the foot, and I, the only guest, at one side. Jamie, in his new dignity as my attendant, stood at my left as instructed and attended to my every want.

Seeing that I ate very little, Dr. DuPree inquired solicitously of my health. I explained how different this fare of vegetables, fowl, fish, and hot breads was from the salt beef and hard tack offered aboard ship.

"Ha!" exclaimed Dr. DuPree. "The food aboard ship is a disgrace! I have often complained to the ships' owners. It has now been discovered that the scurvy, which takes off crew and passengers alike, is from the lack of fresh fruit and vegetables. I have recommended that lemons be taken aboard always.

"Bah!" he continued wrathfully. "There is so much we

don't know about diseases. I have observed the curious fact that people from Africa seem more resistant to the yellow fever than we of the white race. But, to date, no one knows even what causes the disease or how it is spread."

"Do you expect some day to find the answer?" I asked curiously.

There was a sudden stillness. The servants had stopped their ministrations for the moment and were gazing at the doctor. He drew himself even more erect and said solemnly, "Sir, it is the purpose of my life!" Thus saying, he got up and left the room.

Astounded, I looked at my hostess. "I am sorry," I stammered. "It is not a question I should ask, perhaps?"

I saw that sudden tears were in her eyes.

"You could not know, sir, that my mother and my only brother died last year of the yellow fever."

It suddenly became clear to me. "And the room I slept in last night?"

"That was his room. The portrait over the mantel is of him. They said we were much alike."

The puzzling resemblance was now explained. "And the clothes I have on—they were his?"

"Yes, you are somewhat the same age and size."

"How very generous of you and your father!" I exclaimed.

My hostess now rose and led the way to the veranda. The tears still sparkled on her lashes, but she said gravely, "Perhaps, sir, sorrow has made us kinder."

6
The Fair Captain

I must have dozed off in my chair on the veranda because I was brought sharply awake by Jamie's voice in my ear. "Angus! There's surely trouble! Abram has come to tell you something!"

I followed him to the rear veranda. Abram stood at the foot of the steps. He was breathing hard, the sweat shining on his face, as if he had come at a run.

"Boy!" he said, "Marse Heyward sent a message for you."

"Yes, Abram, what is it?" I demanded.

"De slave ship, she gone! But them men, de slavers, make brag in de grogshops alongside de bay that they just touched you before, but—oh, boy!—I fear to say it . . ."

"Go ahead, Abram," said Savannah, who had appeared on the steps beside me.

Abram turned his troubled face to her. "They brag that de *third* time they get him, it be de last!"

"But you said the slave ship was gone! Why should anyone want to kill me?" I demanded.

"They pass de word along, boy. They swear to get you, and they got friends who do it for 'em!"

"This is true, Angus!" said Savannah. "It is a well-known fact that these cutthroats and thieves have a close-knit fraternity. And now, instead of the three who attacked you . . ."

"I have a dozen rascals howling for my blood!" I said bitterly. I remembered the blow that flung me into the bay without warning and the pursuit in the darkness. When would the next blow fall?

Abram was watching me anxiously. "Marse Heyward, he uneasy 'bout you, boy."

I laughed. "And what does he propose to do?"

"He say he got a plan. You to meet him at de barracks."

"At the barracks?"

"He say he think he can help."

I shook my head. No one could help.

Savannah put an urgent hand on my arm. "Angus, I think you should go. Mr. Heyward feels responsible for the attacks on you. Perhaps he can help. Do you feel able to go?"

"Of course!" My pride was touched.

She regarded me with a grave face. "Oh, la! sir! That Scottish pride of yours!"

To my chagrin, I realized that she had selected the very spur that would be most likely to move me.

"You will need some protection from the sun. Wait a moment."

She disappeared within and returning, helped me into a jacket and placed a large straw hat upon my bandaged
· head.

She laughed, "You look like a very angry Scotsman!"

"And a very frightened one," I confessed ruefully.

"Look after him, Abram!"

Abram was enjoying my discomfort. "Yas'm, that surely what I aim to do!"

With Jamie and Savannah watching, I marched off to the barracks with Abram as my guardian.

Mr. Heyward was waiting in the square and greeted me warmly.

"Ah, my dear Mr. Ferguson! Dr. DuPree and Abram

have told me about last night's affair. I am grateful you came off so well."

I bowed, although somewhat stiffly. "Thank you, sir. I owe my coming off to Abram and to Mistress DuPree."

He glanced at Abram's great bulk and his eyes twinkled. "Ah, yes! One would always hope to have Abram around the corner in case of desperate need. I understand that the lady's riding whip also helped."

"It did, indeed, sir. I acknowledge my indebtedness."

He smiled, "Now, let us see if we can get you out of this last threat. Come inside. I have a friend who might help."

At the barracks door Mr. Heyward addressed the two sentries courteously. "Mr. Heyward and Mr. Ferguson to see Captain Stuart. Please announce us."

"Yes, sir!" they chanted in unison. The corporal preceded us, opened a door, and announced our presence in ringing tones. An erect figure rose to greet us, and thus I met the famous Captain John Stuart.

Captain Stuart was the epitome of the colonial officer, erect and splendid in blue coat, facings and breeches, and mirror-bright black boots. His sandy hair was worn unpowdered. A ruddy, deeply lined face spoke of long exposure to an outdoor life.

"Welcome, Mr. Heyward."

I was surprised to hear a Scottish burr in his voice.

"Thank you, Captain. This is the young man I've told you of—Angus Ferguson—only lately come to our shores."

"And stirred up a hornet's nest, I hear!"

His quizzical glance took me in from head to foot. He smiled.

"Is it possible that this is the stout lad who put three cutthroats to flight?"

"I was not entirely alone, Captain Stuart," I protested. "I had some formidable help in the business."

"Modest, too," murmured the captain. "Gentlemen, be seated. Now, Mr. Heyward, you sent me word you needed my help. I am at your service."

"Captain," said Mr. Heyward, "I feel that I am responsible for this lad's safety. He reported to me that living slaves on my vessel *The Indian Queen* were thrown overboard. The captain denies that any such event took place. No one verifies the charge except a small boy who, like Mr. Ferguson here, was aboard *The Wanderer* at the time."

"The captain of *The Wanderer?*"

"He denies it, also."

"Whom do you believe, Mr. Heyward?"

"This lad, sir."

"Against the denial of two experienced captains?"

"Yes."

"What are your reasons?"

"The fact that this lad is a Scotsman, like yourself . . ."

The captain bowed.

"And that he had everything to lose and nothing to gain."

"I understand that two attempts have been made against his life."

"I have it on good authority, captain, that a third attempt is promised. Doubtless, it will be carried out."

"And what would you have me to do?"

"Get him out of Charles Town—immediately!"

I was startled and looked at Mr. Heyward. He caught my glance. His voice was bitter.

"Ah, lad, you think, no doubt, that this danger can be warded off by another fence picket?"

"But to run, Mr. Heyward?"

58

"Aye, I'd have you run—and fast. I want not your death on my conscience!"

The captain sat regarding me, his chin in his hand. No doubt he noted on my face the realization of my predicament.

"What is your opinion, sir?" he asked me.

"It smacks of cowardice, sir."

"Cowardice, my dear sir," said the captain, "is a very different thing from prudence. In the city the whole company of His Majesty's soldiers could not protect you at all times. If you were to leave for a while, however, it is quite likely that the villains who attacked you or their confederates would be found or would go on to other places, less dangerous to them."

"But where would I go, sir?" I asked.

Mr. Heyward turned to the officer. "Captain Stuart, you and your detachment leave tomorrow for the Overhill fort. Could you not employ this lad in some capacity on that expedition? A few peaceful months spent in the Cherokee country would take him out of the present danger, and very likely he can return in safety thereafter."

"An excellent thought," said the captain, "although I cannot promise peaceful months ahead." He turned to me.

"Now, sir," he said. "Let us see how His Majesty can make best use of your talents. It is not often that we engage a lad of your honesty"—he glanced at my bandaged head—"or of your hardihood. Besides these assets, you are a fellow Scot. All these factors are highly commendable!"

I blushed to hear such words used to describe my character, but I had an uneasy feeling that the captain was secretly laughing although his face was grave.

59

He continued, "At present, we are desperate for recruits who know something about cannon."

I thought of the merciless hazing that the sentries had put me through and shook my head.

"My father raised me for the cloth, sir, and I know nothing of guns and cannon. I fear that I have very little of the proper knowledge to make my way in the New World."

"Very few of us arrived on these shores with such knowledge. It must be acquired here."

Mr. Heyward spoke up. "Would there be any chance of his being employed as a scrivener?"

"An excellent suggestion!" said the captain. "Mr. Elliot, who furnishes the packtrain that goes with us, is hard put to keep his accounts straight. Captain Demere also needs someone to help occasionally with the dispatches. His reports are often written at night, and candlelight is hard on his eyesight. Yes, I think there is a possibility of usefulness there."

"Good!" said Mr. Heyward. "Then the matter is settled."

He and the captain rose, and I with them, grateful that the two gentlemen had concerned themselves with my affairs. Stammering, I tried to tell them so, but they brushed aside my thanks and made light of their help.

"You will report here at eight of the clock," directed the captain.

"Yes, sir!"

"However, there is the matter of your security tonight."

"I shall be safe enough in Dr. DuPree's home."

The captain shook his head. "The governor and Assembly do not care for a disturbance of the peace. I fear I must insist on two soldiers accompanying you. Tell

Dr. DuPree we regret the necessity, but they must stand guard tonight."

"My thanks for your assistance, Captain Stuart." Mr. Heyward said. "Count me your debtor in the future."

The captain bowed and dismissed us.

"'Tis glad I am to have made your acquaintance, lad." Mr. Heyward said to me when we were outside the barracks. "This Guinea business"—he mused a moment sadly—"tars all it touches. I've no doubt that a price will be exacted of us someday. God bless you!"

And he walked quickly away.

Abram, waiting outside the barracks, had caught the gentle tones of his voice. "I think he like you, boy!"

"And I am beginning to like him, Abram. I thought him a fearfully angry man when first we met."

"Most folks improve on 'quaintance, boy," he said, but he laughed and shook his head as he amended his statement. "But some just get worser!"

He was overjoyed to learn that I would be assigned to the packtrain, since he too would be going.

Followed by two soldiers, I returned to the house on Meeting Street. I felt as conspicuous as a felon being escorted to the gallows.

Jamie was wild with excitement at our appearance. One of the soldiers stationed himself at the front door and the other at the rear, putting the whole household in an uproar. I never felt more foolish in my life to be the cause of such a commotion. My host and his daughter were of the opinion that I must do exactly as the captain and Mr. Heyward had urged.

Savannah now gave her prompt attention to making me ready for my journey. Abram had found my seabag, discarded in my flight, and brought it to the house. Now it was pressed into service again. The original items it held—my father's gift of a Bible and my mother's last lovingly made shirt—were first put in. The shirt had been carefully laundered and ironed.

My hostess insisted that I continue to use the garments her brother had worn and added a soft deerskin hunting shirt. My heavy wool jacket and breeches, washed and ironed, were put in. My plaid, too, had been freshly washed.

Dr. DuPree did me the honor to give me an hour of his valuable time, receiving me in his study. He explained the country I should traverse, using a map mounted on a wall. He pointed out the trading path to the Cherokee country and the rivers by which it was approached.

Dusk fell, and gradually the house was put to rights for the night. Jamie begged to sleep again across my threshold, declaring that the vigilance of the soldiers was not to be trusted. I permitted it, quite touched by his solicitude, only specifying that he use my plaid as his bed.

When the first light of morning came, I wakened and dressed for my journey. I stood for a long while by the window where the early morning breezes blew the curtains and wondered if I should ever again be surrounded by the peace and delightful order of the DuPree household. The eyes of the laughing boy of the portrait followed me as I left the room.

Dr. DuPree, Savannah, and Jamie, with the servants clustering behind them, bade me farewell. As I walked down the street, followed by the two soldiers, I wished that I might have remained there the rest of my life.

The barracks were busy. Men ran in every direction assembling gear and weapons. The officers and most of the men were extremely military and well turned out, but the newer recruits looked like ruffians just off a ship's deck. Later, I found out my impressions were correct.

Any sailor who knew something of gunnery and of handling ropes was hired, and a rough crew indeed they seemed to be.

Captain Stuart directed me to go to the wharf to assist Mr. Elliot in getting the packtrain on its way.

From a distance I was hailed by Abram, busy loading the horses. At my question, he assured me those small, but sturdy creatures would be able to travel under their heavy loads. A wooden frame was fastened to each animal's back and bales of merchandise were carefully balanced on either side.

I had not counted on the smells and noise of the packtrain. Bells fastened to each horse's neck gave out a constant jangle. The drovers ranged alongside with enormous whips to urge the horses on.

The train finally got underway. The shouts of the drovers, the crack and hiss of whips, the wild jangle of the bells were all but deafening.

"Boy, you get used to it!" Abram laughed as we took our place.

I doubted that, but shouldered my plaid and bulging seabag and trudged alongside.

The column of marching soldiers and mounted officers had joined us and moved ahead. To the cadence of beating drums we were on our way to the Overhill fort!

7

On the Trading Path

The journey into the Overhill Cherokee country was the strangest I had ever been on. I was familiar with the wild and lonely highlands of Scotland, over which I had roamed freely from my earliest years, yet here were lands vaster, wilder, and more beautiful than any I had dreamed of.

For many days we traveled along the banks of lazy rivers, through marshes and cane brakes, as the natives called the impenetrable lush, green growth. Huge trees sheltered us from the hot sun. Beneath their tangled canopies, streamers of a curious gray, feathery moss blew in the wind. At times the perfume of huge white blossoms high in glossy trees all but suffocated me.

We plodded beneath this steaming tropical greenery, bells jangling on the horses' necks, drovers' whips cracking, the soldiers moving in steady step set to the rhythm of the drums, with abrupt commands occasionally ringing out like gunshots.

Along the way our Indian escorts joined us, ranging along our extended column. Silently and without haste, they appeared suddenly out of the shadows—shadows themselves.

"Cherokees," explained Abram. Then he added for my information, "Proud! Proud as de devil!"

At that very moment a lad of about my own age came past us. For a moment his dark eyes stared into mine, then he passed on down the column.

"Did he understand what you just said, Abram?" I asked.

"No, think not."

I was not so sure. "He looked directly at me, then dropped his eyes."

"Ain't manners among 'em to look straight at a fella."

There had been such a look of scorn in the dark eyes that had confronted me that I was sure he understood the tone of Abram's comment, if not the words.

"Do any of them speak English?" This time I looked carefully about me, before I asked my question.

"Big Chief Attakullakulla—him as is Cap'n Stuart's friend—he speak good English. Traders marry Indian wives, and some of them speak English."

"How then do we communicate with them?"

"Sign language."

"What's sign language? I've never heard of it."

Abram laughed, "Me, I not so good, but sometime at camp time, I show you."

Stinging clouds of insects hung about us on the trail and made life miserable for horses and men alike. The drovers showed me how to smudge my face and arms with mud from the riverbanks to discourage the insects somewhat.

The only real relief came at night when we were free to plunge into the river and thus cool our tired limbs. Refreshed, we gathered about the many small fires that shone among the trees. Here food was cooked and served in common pots. Afterwards, each man spread blanket or boughs beneath him and lay down for the night's rest.

To my ears, the nights were loud with unaccustomed noises. The tethered animals moved constantly as they fed upon the cane and grass of the riverbanks. Birds of the night called and answered. Unseen animals snorted in the underbrush and then crashed away. Once wolves howled long and fiercely, and a wakeful drover started up and grasped his gun to put them to flight. A sinewy figure grappled with him. The scuffle brought another drover who translated for the Cherokee. "The wolves are the hunting dogs of the Great Kanati. Do not touch them!"

As we left the flat land and followed the trail winding through the gently rising hills, we abandoned the deep shade of the great trees. The burning rays of the sun were only partially obstructed. In the heat my face flamed as red as my hair.

That night when we made camp I was so miserable that I had no desire for food. Abram was alarmed and insisted that I drink a fragrant tea that he brewed for me. It was good, but like nothing I had ever tasted. He said it was made by boiling the roots of a native shrub called sassafras.

I lay on the river bank, too spent to move. Suddenly the young Cherokee I had noticed before came to look down at me.

He raised his eyes from my heavy leather boots and looked in my face briefly, then dropped his gaze. Coming to some decision, he gestured for me to remove the boots. I did so and found my feet chafed and swollen. I was directed by his silent gesture to cool them in the small stream we had been following.

The relief was immediate. He disappeared for a little and, returning, knelt and wrapped about my feet the dry, gray moss I had observed earlier. He drew over this a pair of soft leather shoes and bound them about the ankles with leather thongs.

I thanked him gratefully. Then I saw an exercise of the

curious communication that Abram had mentioned—sign language.

Abram, who stood near, gestured to himself and to me in a way that was puzzling to me but apparently meant something to the young Cherokee, for he responded with other gestures.

Abram looked at me. "I tell him, boy, we friends. He ask our names."

Abram touched his breast then pronounced, slowly, "Abram!" The young man looked puzzled, and Abram repeated the performance. Then he touched my shoulder and pronounced carefully, "An-gus! An-gus!"

The Cherokee pointed to Abram and to me and carefully repeated Abram's syllables. I confess I could not make out a resemblance, but Abram professed himself delighted.

Then Abram gestured toward the youth and asked his name. Comprehending the question, the Cherokee drew himself up, pronounced a word proudly, and stalked off.

Abram chuckled as he sat down.

"My sign language not too good. He say he Cherokee, and that all I get!"

Nevertheless, we felt that we had a friend among our escorts and looked for him often.

Abram found me another pair of the soft leather shoes that my friend had given me. They were called moccasins, he informed me. A second pair was necessary, since the pair worn during a day had to be carefully dried that night over a fire. Failing a fire, I could carry the damp pair inside my shirt, thus making that extra pair soft, dry, and ready for use.

Every day I spent on the trail, I found the way less arduous, and I felt myself growing stronger and more knowledgeable.

We came at last to the outpost Fort Prince George and marched within its palisades. Everything about it looked as if it had been hastily constructed. Stores and supplies of all kinds were kept here—many destined for the Overhill fort, but not yet carried thither because of the great lack of pack animals.

Here I saw the special care given to the supplies of ammunition. The boxes containing this material had been carried on the packhorses with the other supplies. But now two soldiers guarded each box and were relieved at regular intervals. This was to guard against any sudden theft by the Cherokees who had incessant need for it and equally to guard against the possibility of fire.

The supplies for Fort Prince George were now unloaded and given over to the care of the garrison. The remaining bales and boxes were repacked for our final destination. Many boxes previously stored at the outpost were added to our horses' loads.

We left early the next morning, the drovers grumbling because of the early start, but Captain Stuart's peremptory orders admitted no argument.

Several days later we came upon our first close look at the mountains, stretching across our way to the north. In the shifting cloud patterns the shades of green, blue, and lavender changed before our eyes.

"There!" said Abram happily. "High mountains, big trees, cold rivers. Mighty pretty! And them rivers go west, nobody know how far."

"You love this country, Abram," I remarked. "You must have seen it many times."

"I know this path like one of them Cherokee! I could find it in the dark! Only, hope never have to!"

"You must be an experienced woodsman, Abram."

"Fair. Not good as Cherokee."

68

From now on the heat of the early fall days grew more bearable. The nights were cool, and the heat of the cooking fires was welcome.

As our path climbed even higher, the character of the trees changed. The glossy-leaved, flowering trees gave way to pines and evergreens. Hawks, ravens, and huge soaring birds I took for vultures scanned our progress from the skies. Abram insisted that the big birds were called buzzards and that their appearance was a sign of bad luck.

One night as we settled down to sleep I heard a subdued drumming—a rhythm that wandered a bit and then settled down to an insistent throbbing. The men grew quiet as the drumbeat pulsed through the night. Then a strong voice took up a chant and rose steadily—proud and warlike—ending in a sudden yell followed by silence. I walked to where Abram sat crouched over the regimental drum, his large hands caressing it. He looked up at me and smiled.

"Where did you learn that song?" I asked.

He shrugged. "Little old song. Ain't nothing."

"Did your father teach it to you?"

He wrinkled his brow in an elaborate show of remembering. "Mebbe. Africa rising in my blood."

He smiled and settled down to sleep. I lay and looked up at the stars for a long time. The drumbeat was still ringing in my mind. How had Abram come to this strange land? For that matter, how had any of us arrived here, to lie under these strange stars?

Then one day before us stretched the valley of the Tennessee, the river of the Cherokees. Its clear waters flowed to the north and west. The gentle ridges of the valley were covered with huge trees. The level lands were green, checkered with fields and garden patches near the clusters of houses.

Small naked children ran to see us as we passed, alerted by the sounds of our march. Each boy clutched a bow and carried a quiver of arrows on his back.

As we approached the bark and wattle houses, we saw the other inhabitants busy about small fires or occupied in tending the fields. They stopped to watch us go by, but no voice was raised in greeting and no smiles crossed their faces.

"Abram," I said, "aren't they happy to see us? I see no sign of welcome."

"Manners," replied Abram. "They's very mannerly and dignified. Besides"—he grinned at me—"this their country. We the strangers."

He was right—we were the strangers. It was a new thought to me.

I had been so busy by day and so weary by night that I had given only fleeting thoughts to my friends of Charles Town. Abram reminded me that when we reached the Overhill fort the packtrain would return along the trading path, he with it, and that he would be happy to carry any message I cared to send to the DuPrees.

Abram assured me that if he had not belonged to "Marse Benn" he would have chosen to belong to Dr. DuPree.

"Would not you rather choose to be a free man, Abram?" I asked.

He glanced at me sharply and was silent for a bit. Then he said, "I free in my mind, boy!"

At dusk we pulled aside into a meadow, or savannah as it was called, and made camp near the house of a trader of the region. His small brood of children swarmed about, not distinguishable from the children of the villages. The

trader's house and outbuildings were large and com-
modious, the house neat, and the outbuildings bursting
with stores of food and trading goods. Cattle and pigs
were penned behind rude fences or ran wild in the woods
about us.

That night we had a feast. Two large bears had been
killed, and the inhabitants of the nearby village presented
them to the soldiers and traders. The baskets of beans
and squash brought by the women were a welcome relief
from our customary diet of dried beef and corn cakes.

My duties as clerk for Mr. Elliot now began and took a
part of each day. At every trader's post bales and boxes
were unloaded. A careful record was kept of the contents
and tallied against that of the trader.

At our last camp before entering the fort I wandered
from fire to fire watching the excitement and unusual
activity. Captain Stuart went from one group of soldiers
to another. Nothing escaped his sharp eye. Belts were
whitened, boots were shined, even the metal of harness
and guns was polished again and again until it shone.

Early the next morning the detachments stood for the
roll call and then stepped out smartly to the cadence of
the drum. The pack horses and supplies followed more
slowly.

The end of our long journey was at hand!

8
Fort Loudoun

And so it was that my first sight of the Overhill fort was a brave sight indeed! The long column approached through a small valley, the soldiers marching to a brisk drumbeat, their uniforms brilliant in the bright sun. Ahead, to the left of the river, loomed the palisades of the fort, rising above the earthen ramparts. Small cannons were mounted at the elevated corners. Above it all, the red and blue of the English flag snapped in the breeze.

As the soldiers came to the walls, the large double gate facing our path swung open, and the column marched within.

Inside, I stood open-mouthed and observed the interior of this busy fort. Opposite the gates we had entered rose a ridge. On this elevation stood two small huts that I guessed to be the officers' quarters, for sentries stood guard, and there the flag was raised.

To the left rose wooden barracks in step-stone fashion, each with a stone chimney attached. In the open corner beyond this, a few horses were tethered. Beyond was a curious small-roofed structure, built half underground. To my immediate left was a roofed well, and to my right was a large and noisy blacksmith shop. It had a roof, but was open on two sides.

Here it was that Mr. Elliot instructed me to set up a temporary office. Into the clangor and bustle of the blacksmith's forge, I brought a rough table provided for the purpose and set up my employer's accounts. The drovers brought the horses here and unloaded the packs.

The ammunition came first and was carefully unloaded, checked by Mr. Elliot, and given over to the care
of the quartermaster and the soldiers who carried it away
for storage. Boxes and packs of food were next broken
open, checked, and turned over to the sergeant: flour,
salt, beef, tea, sugar, and—I thought of Dr. DuPree's
lecture—lemons! Salt was unloaded in surprising quan-
tity.

Then came clothing, blankets, crockery, and all the
many items necessary for the running of this large
household.

When the last of the military supplies was bestowed,
we began unloading, checking off, and setting aside
boxes and packs designated for the Indian trade. Freed of
their cargo, the small packhorses were led back out the
large double gate to be tethered, fed, and tended. The
drovers now shouldered the trade packages and carried
them out a small gate to my right, beyond which ran the
river.

Cleared of my duties, I walked out the river gate to see
the disposition of the trade goods.

The palisades of the fort were formed of large stripped
logs, their bases set into the ground and the tops
sharpened to a point. They were bound together tightly
and leaned out at an oblique angle, supported by earthen
ramparts. Below lay a large dry ditch separated from the
ramparts by a hedge of small trees and shrubs bristling
with huge thorns.

Outside, the short path divided. The branch in front of
me ran directly to the river, deep and dark at this point,
where canoes were drawn up on the bank. These, too,
were guarded.

The other path turned upward. Following it, I mounted
a small platform just outside the ramparts. To my

surprise, here underneath a shed, was set up a complete small store with a busy forge at one side. A small, round, leather-lunged woman presided over this establishment.

Arms akimbo, she turned and regarded me alertly. "And who may you be, my lad? It's easy to see you're no soldier of the king!"

I bowed. "Angus Ferguson, ma'am."

"And, by the way your tongue rolls your name around, a Scotsman and a Highlander?"

"Yes, ma'am."

"Well, well! A babe lost in the Cherokee wilds! Will wonders never cease!"

I could not take offense, since she was so small and fierce.

"My name is Dorothy Bacon," she continued. "My husband is Corporal Bacon, as you may have seen about the fort. You must be the new boy as is employed by Master Elliot?"

"Yes, ma'am. I'm also to help Captain Demere when he needs me."

"Well, Captain Demere—this here fort's commanding officer—'as told me to run this trading post for the Cherokee. He don't want none a'slipping into the fort and stealing his ammunition."

I thought that the captain had chosen wisely to select such a termagant to manage the trade goods.

"Well, why are you standing there, young sir? You are to help the captain, ain't ye? Get busy and earn your pay!"

Thus admonished, I set to, at the lady's direction. Two soldiers had already been working, and Mistress Bacon kept the three of us busy, breaking open the newly arrived barrels and packs and adding their contents to the shelves and chests underneath the shed's roof. It puzzled me that here was a second forge and smith. But I put the question off until later, when perhaps the lady's tongue had lost its edge!

Nevertheless, one question popped out, in spite of me. "Why do they call this the Overhill fort?" I asked in an unlucky moment.

The full scorn of Mistress Bacon's countenance was turned upon me.

"The name of His Majesty's fort is Fort Loudoun, me lad, and let's hear no more talk of the Overhill fort! 'Tis for the ignorant, lazy Charles Town folk, who speak of this as belonging to the Overhill Cherokee, seeing as how they live beyond the mountains. 'Tis named in honor of the famous Lord Loudoun, and let not ye be a'saying ye never heard tell of him!"

I shook my head. My ignorance in military matters was a deep affront to my informer, and I resolved to keep a quiet tongue in my head thereafter!

At day's end Mistress Bacon locked her stores and left them to the care of a guard.

"You'll make a fair hand, lad," she said not unkindly as she left.

When Abram came to call me to the night's meal, I asked him where her home was, and he told me that the soldiers who had wives and families with them lived outside the fort in small houses near the river.

He and I ate our supper inside the fort with the drovers and then spread our blankets beneath the blacksmith's roof.

On the morrow Mr. Elliot assembled his horses and drovers, and Abram came to bid me good-bye. I was to stay and keep the accounts at Mistress Bacon's store.

I was sorry to see Abram go, for it was to him that I applied for the answers to my numerous questions. He promised to give my regards to my friends on Meeting Street, and happy to be on the trail, he went out the east gate with the noisy throng.

Mistress Bacon set me promptly to work on Mr. Elliot's accounts. Here I saw firsthand the many trade items that the Cherokee had come to depend upon and were willing to barter hides and game for. Some of them seemed to me to be particularly odd, but I was assured that those very ones were important items of commerce. Some were small jars of paint—black, yellow, and vermilion. Seeing my puzzled looks at these objects, Madam Storekeeper burst into a hearty laugh.

"Have you never seen an Indian warrior dressed up?" she asked.

"I've only seen a few Indians, and they were our escorts on the trading path."

"Well, this paint is to make 'em feared by their enemies."

Gay lengths of calico was another popular item, bought to make petticoats for the women and shirts for the men. Beads, lace, and ribbons were also desired—the beads of bright colors being used as adornment and money. Hawkbells—small, bronze tinkling things—were bought to adorn and fringe clothing. Iron kettles were also much in demand.

"But what these Cherokee want most of all," continued my instructor, "are guns and ammunition."

She pointed to the forge, now busy. "That's for the Cherokee guns. They're old guns and always need repair. Every warrior wants a gun, you must know."

The arrival and departure of the packhorse train had been noted for many miles, and now began a constant stream of Cherokee men and women to purchase. Mistress Bacon knew them all and kept up a steady chatter with them, whether they understood her or not. She was adept at comprehending their gestures and kept me busy recording their selections.

"How are they to pay for them, Mistress Bacon?" I asked when my curiosity got the better of me.

"They'll bring in hides after the big winter hunt," said she, never pausing in her job. "My land, boy! You have a lot to learn! They'll sell us beans and corn, and things they can pick up in the woods—game, nuts, turkeys— mighty good eating! We'll put some fat on yer bones while ye're here!

"You're as thin as a rail in a snake fence!" she scolded. "Your folks sure didn't feed you, or maybe you've run away from home?"

"No, ma'am. My parents are dead, and I just arrived recently in Charles Town on *The Wanderer* out of Glasgow."

"My land! No wonder you don't know your way around! I've followed the army many a year with my man and we've been here since the fort was built, so if you want to know anything about this place, just ask Dorothy Bacon."

I promised to do so, reflecting that her sharp manner covered a warm heart. Nevertheless, her caustic tongue never ceased, and I observed that she got instant obedience from one and all. I doubted that even the officers could stand against her.

From the first night that I slept within the fort, I had known of the continual activity of the soldiers. As I lay upon my blanket on this second night, I learned that the officers particularly labored long into the night. Candles were lit within the captains' quarters, and through an open doorway I caught glimpses of the two men at a table amid papers, pens, and inkpots. The candles burned far

77

into the night. Before the early light, a soldier was summoned to the door, and given papers. He rode off through the gate, the rhythm of his horse's gallop growing fainter as he hurried down the trading path to Charles Town.

I thought again of the city by the harbor and of a certain fenced garden and of the generous hearts and kind faces therein. When would I see that delightful place again?

Fort Loudoun—I was never again to call it the Overhill fort, mindful of Mistress Bacon's admonition—was a beehive of activity. I seldom saw the officers since I was busy at the trading post, and they kept to a strict routine of duties within the fort. Captain Stuart was kind enough to inquire after my welfare. I caught occasional glimpses of the commanding officer, Captain Paul Demere, who was called "the dark captain" to distinguish him from "the fair captain," Captain Stuart. I learned that the soldiers stood in considerable awe of these two men.

To me the most interesting figure of all was Mr. Shorey, a dark, morose individual who served as the linguister, or interpreter, to the fort. It was whispered among the soldiers that he was the highest paid, next to the captains. I was never able to learn whether he was employed as a soldier—regular British Army as was Captain Demere or South Carolina Provincial as was Captain Stuart—or as a civilian.

In whatever category he was hired, he was his own man. He dressed in hunting shirt, breeches, and moccasins; spoke a half-dozen Indian languages; was married to a Cherokee; and, according to the soldiers, had eyes in the back of his head and was in league with the devil.

He would appear silently, seat himself at a soldier's fire,

share the food, and then, without a word of thanks or farewell, leave abruptly. His comings and goings were subject only to the captains' directions. I was told that he, like the soldiers who were married, lived near the fort.

One night he appeared without warning and sat at my side as I was watching the night's activities of the fort. He did not look at me, but sat balanced on his heels, as I had seen the Indians do.

"New?" he inquired.

"Yes, sir."

"Where from?"

"Scotland, sir."

"Why here?"

"I got in trouble in Charles Town, sir."

"You the boy reported *The Indian Queen?*"

"Yes, sir."

"Lucky. Hear the slavers nearly killed you."

"Yes, sir. They tried."

"Abram said Captain Stuart brought you to get you out of trouble. That true?"

"Yes, sir. The owner of the *The Queen* asked him to do so."

"Well, my lad, you jumped from the frying pan into the fire."

I was puzzled at this peculiar statement. "What do you mean, sir?"

"Cherokees are just itching to go on the warpath. They'd prefer to start right here." His glance took in the walls of the fort.

"I thought they were friends, sir."

"They near about changed their minds. French send in messengers to tell 'em how nice it would be if all the English was back down in Charles Town. The murdering conduct of us English don't help."

He laughed shortly.

"French offer good money for English scalps." His glance took me in briefly. "Wouldn't surprise me if there were a special price to be gotten for yours. Ain't often a body gets a chance at such red hair."

I thought of my friend of the trading path.

"Surely not all the Cherokee are against us, sir."

"Old Chief Attakullakulla—him they call the Little Carpenter—he's still our friend. I don't know as we have many more friends than him and his family."

"Can you tell me the name of a young man about my age and height who was kind to me on the trading path? He gave me a pair of moccasins."

"Sounds like Tsalohi. He belongs to Attakullakulla's family."

"He seems different from other Cherokee?"

"He understands English. Won't speak it."

"He does?"

"He and his sister lived with my wife for a while. They're orphans."

"Oh, that explains it—his understanding English. I thought he was laughing at me, once or twice."

"They all do—laugh like crazy. They think white men are very funny. Never let us know, though." He rose and prepared to depart. "I think we're funny too."

As he left I shook my head. No wonder the soldiers gave the man credit for being in league with supernatural powers!

9
The Dark Captain

One morning I reported to Mistress Bacon as usual. But her noisy presence was much quieter this particular morning.

"Keep a civil tongue in your head, lad," she advised me. "Them Cherokee is spoiling for a fight!" And she gestured to where three men waited silently. Each clutched a gun. They did not move, but their eyes followed us as Mistress Bacon and I set up shop for the day. They were not there for the clothing or adornments I felt sure.

Mistress Bacon said loudly for their benefit, "Private Smith will be here directly!"

They made no sound.

Again Mistress Bacon's voice was raised in explanation. "The gunsmith is late this morning!"

Still there was no response. We continued to work, although the mounting tension in the air could almost be felt.

The gunsmith, Private Thomas Smith, came whistling as he walked through the river gate. Silently, the three warriors extended their weapons.

He examined their guns. I could see that they were quite old and in bad repair. He looked at the Cherokees, and said, "I cannot mend!"

They understood him, for the leader looked searchingly at him, as if to determine the truth or falsity of the statement, and then deliberately spat at the gunsmith's feet.

"Angus," said the gunsmith, his voice shaking in anger, "get the linguister, and be quick about it!"

I sped on my errand and returned with Mr. Shorey.

A long monologue followed, Mr. Shorey explaining something carefully to our visitors. At the end, the leader said just one word. I took it to be the Cherokee equivalent for "You mend!"

Mr. Shorey sighed. He turned to the still indignant gunsmith. "Smith, you've got to mend these guns or there'll be a war on, right now!"

"Ain't worth it! It'll take me all day."

"This man," Mr. Shorey indicated the leader, "is a head man of Citico. He's Tuskeegi-Tahee, and he is not fond of the English. It's very important to please him."

"I don't care if he's the devil himself. I don't take no orders from a Cherokee. Captain Demere gives the orders here!"

Mr. Shorey turned and reentered the fort. He was back shortly.

"Captain Demere's compliments to Private Smith, and you're to repair those guns if it takes till kingdom come!"

The gunsmith started wrathfully to work. "Shorey, get that blacksmith to send me two helpers. I can't abide them Indians all day!"

Mistress Bacon had been silent for once during this scene.

"Angus, me lad," she sighed, "I'm plumb wore out, as if I'd done a day's washing! Can't you sing us a song, mayhap to get them fellers in a better mood?"

I had never been noted for my ability to entertain, but in the interest of peace, I began to recollect verses taught me long ago and gradually broke into the full rendition of "The Gypsy Lad" as I went about my duties.

With my singing and the busy clamor of the forge,

attended now by Private Smith and his two helpers, the place was certainly noisy, if not cheerful. The three Cherokees sat silent spectators of all that went on.

It came to me that there had been no Indian women at the store in some time. They had been frequent visitors, smiling and quiet, taking their time in making their selections.

"Where are the women?" I whispered to Mistress Bacon. "I miss them."

"They got other things on their minds," rejoined Mistress Bacon cryptically.

"What do you mean?" I asked.

"My guess is that their menfolk is just a'spoiling for a fight, like them fellers yonder, and their wives is probably getting in the corn and beans and looking forward to a hard winter."

I shivered. I hoped she was no prophet.

An orderly came looking for me.

"Ferguson, Captain Stuart says you are to report to him and Captain Demere, soon as you can."

What would the two captains want with me?

The orderly looked me over. "Ain't you got nothing beside that hunting shirt?"

"Yes."

"Get it on. The captains are particular!"

Thus warned, I dragged out my seabag and, borrowing a gourd full of soap from Mistress Bacon, retired to a secluded pool in the river. Here I soaped myself from head to foot, plunged in, and, thus refreshed, dried myself and got into the clothes that Dr. DuPree and Savannah had given me. A fresh pair of moccasins did duty.

Returning, I found a comb among the store's shelves and attempted some order in my hair. Mistress Bacon added the finishing touch of a thong to club my hair and stood back.

"You've grown a bit since you've been here, Angus, and now you do look like a gentleman."

"Thank you, ma'am."

"Keep away from them Cherokee girls, laddie!" she admonished.

I blushed, and she laughed.

"I'll wash your hunting shirt for you," she volunteered as I left.

Nevertheless, it was a Cherokee woman I met as I approached the captains' quarters. She looked at me alertly and then glanced modestly down. I turned to watch her as she was let out the river gate. She was attractive with her free carriage, bright clothes, and dark braids.

Captain Stuart was at the door and ushered me within.

"Captain Demere, this is Angus Ferguson of Scotland, as you may know when he speaks. He was recommended to me by two citizens of Charles Town. They are both known to you—Dr. Jarrell DuPree and Mr. John Heyward."

I bowed. Captain Demere, seated behind the table, looked me over from head to foot. If Captain Stuart were the *beau ideal* of the colonial officer, here was his dark British counterpart, less affable, but somehow more elegant.

"Captain Stuart tells me that you have conducted your business as clerk to Monsieur Elliot in satisfactory fashion."

In his turn of phrase and the curious accent of his syllables, I heard hints of another speech learned before English. He was a Frenchman even though he wore the scarlet of His Majesty's regulars.

I glanced at Captain Stuart.

The Dark Captain

"I am pleased to have met with Captain Stuart's approval, sir!"

Captain Demere looked at me again, doubtfully. "Captain," he said to the other, "he is very young, I am sure!"

"But he can be relied upon, I take my oath," Captain Stuart said.

The captain shrugged. "I need help in the business of clerking. I must chance you."

"Yes, sir!"

"You understand that nothing—not the smallest detail!—you learn here is to be repeated to anyone!"

And so my new duties began. I had much to learn, but the two captains were patient. Daily, I came to admire their concern and dedication.

When first I caught sight of the bright uniforms and confident bearing of the soldiers, I had thought that soldiering must surely be a fine business. Perhaps it might be thrilling to march into battle with flags flying and drums beating—provided, of course, that one were the victor and the bloodshed all upon the enemy's side. Now I began to alter my earlier opinion. Here I was privy to the many chores and burdens of soldiers and officers alike. The petty and demanding details of His Majesty's service were onerous: Water—where was it, and was it sufficient? Ammunition—how much was needed, and where could more be had? Food, medicine, clothing, and shoes— where were they to come from, and how long would it take to get them?

I began to understand the reasons for the unceasing movement and activity that centered here in the captains' quarters. Even in this remote vastness far from the battles around Lake George and the Mohawk Valley, the winds of war blew about our ears.

85

From every quarter came intelligence of French influence reaching from Quebec to New Orleans. Here I heard of great armies and navies sent to India, to Canada, to confront the enemy! I became familiar with names I'd never heard of—Montcalm, Wolfe, Clive, Amherst, Forbes, Bouquet.

From here went almost daily reports to the royal governor and to the Assembly in Charles Town of information affecting the colony of South Carolina.

After long hours of dictation had been taken and dispatches readied for the next express, I would lie upon my blanket and sleep as heavily as if I had been laboring in the smithy.

10
The Council House

The young Cherokee woman I had noticed in the fort now came frequently. Her name was Nanye'hi, and she was of Attakullakulla's family. She also spoke English and acted as an interpreter for her people. Her friendly regard for the British was undoubted, and what she had to say was valuable.

Information came daily, through her and through others, of increasing dissatisfaction among the Cherokees. Those against the English were now firmly in control of the Cherokee nation's policies. Only Attakullakulla and a pitiful few held out for friendship.

The year before, Cherokees had been killed in Virginia as they returned to the Overhills from service as scouts for the English army. To avenge their death, settlers had been killed in the western Carolinas. Outraged farmers and settlers struck back. Deaths among settlers and Cherokees mounted.

One day an express came riding to the captains' door with a dispatch that was to change all our lives—the Cherokee chiefs were summoned to Charles Town to meet with the governor.

"Where will it end?" demanded a distraught Captain Stuart.

"I see no help for it," shrugged Captain Demere. "You must take the linguister with you and carry the message to the principal council house at Chota. The Cherokee are to meet the governor on October 18 at Charles Town."

"And what if the Cherokee won't go?"

"Then we sell them no more ammunition."

"The governor knows as well as we do, Demere, that in that event the French will be happy to supply them."

"It is a long way to the Alabama fort. We would hope that the French have only enough ammunition for their own use. Nevertheless, you must carry the message immediately. Take Adamson with you"—and catching sight of me—"Ferguson, if he wishes."

Captain Stuart addressed me, "I cannot command you to go, you understand?"

"I'd like to go, sir! I've never seen a council house ceremony."

"Go, by all means," Captain Demere said with a smile. "Take thought to be attired as impressively as possible. We will offend the Cherokees if we do not properly realize the dignity of the occasion."

Mistress Bacon laundered my one linen shirt, and she lent me a fringed sash to wear about my waist.

"Now, me lad, a hat for you!"

She rummaged in the boxes of her store and came up with a three-cornered hat that sat grandly on my head. One of the soldiers insisted on my wearing his tall black boots. Thus attired, I waited at the river landing for Captain Stuart. We were joined by Lieutenant Adamson and Mr. Shorey and four soldiers, who would row us.

The captain had sent runners ahead and when we drew up with great fanfare to the landing at Chota, the capital of the Cherokee nation, we were led immediately to the council house, a large structure with rounded rooflines, as of an enormous overturned basket. Set upon a raised mound of earth, it faced a plaza packed bare by many feet.

Within the council house, raised seats for the chief men of the nation stood before the ceremonial fire that burned in the center of the room. Around the sides rose tiers of benches occupied by the warriors, each wearing many symbols of his exploits. As guests of honor, we were seated directly in front of the chiefs.

It was hot, by reason of the fire and the presence of many people, but I noticed Captain Stuart made no concession to the sweat trickling down his face. Seeing such an example, I dared give no hint of my own discomfort.

Mr. Shorey told me in a low voice the names and positions of the head men.

"In the center—the three white seats are their emblems of authority—is Kuhna-gatota."

This chief sat tall and impassive as a statue carved out of dark wood.

"He takes the place of Connecorte, the principal chief who is dying."

"On the left is Willenawa, the war chief. Behind him is Oconostota, the great warrior."

Both were equally impassive.

"On the right is Attakullakulla, the peace chief."

So this was the famous chief my father had seen many years ago. He was smaller than the others, and his features were remarkably delicate. Despite his size, however, he was a man of manifest authority.

Strict silence was observed. Food was now brought by the women and offered on mats and baskets placed before the guests. The food was good—deer meat, beans, squash, and corn cakes. We ate without speaking, fingers serving for forks. When the food was taken away, Captain Stuart sent around a large napkin for us to wipe our hands upon.

Kuhna-gatota then filled the ceremonial pipe with tobacco and, drawing a coal from the fire, lighted it. He silently blew a bit of smoke in the four directions of the compass.

He next passed it to Captain Stuart, who puffed upon it, and then to Attakullakulla. From his hand it passed back and forth until all visitors had been honored. The circle of warriors completed passing the pipe until it came at last to the war chief. All this was carried on in silence, each man looking steadfastly before him, as if in meditation.

Now began the talks. Captain Stuart arose and, with Mr. Shorey interpreting, addressed himself to the principal chiefs. He conveyed to his friends, the chiefs of the great Cherokee nation, His Excellency the Royal Governor's invitation to talk about some recent unhappy affairs in which his friends the Cherokee were involved. He hoped the chiefs and headmen would meet him on October 18 at Charles Town.

When the captain seated himself, Kuhna-gatota arose, Mr. Shorey interpreting in English for our benefit. Kuhna-gatota was astonished at the demand of his brother the governor! Everyone knew renegade Creeks and Choctaws were about. If any Cherokee warriors had taken a hand in the affairs, it was no doubt in self-defense since the whole world knew of the peaceful intent of the Cherokee nation. He, Kuhna-gatota, would consult with his warriors and chiefs, and, if it met with their approval, he would accept the invitation to the talk.

Then he added a parting retort: He was sure the Great King Over the Water did not know of the actions of his governor. Everyone knew that Charles Town was a source of lies!

Silence followed this speech.

Captain Stuart arose and courteously took his leave. We followed him out of the council house, walked

90

through the village where silent women and children watched us, and got into the canoe to return to the fort. As we swept down the river, I turned to look back. I was met by the furious gaze of the captain, who had been last to embark.

"Keep your face to the front, sir!" he commanded. "Do you want the Cherokees to see that we fear their arrows in our backs?"

We rowed back in complete silence. As we got out at the landing, Captain Stuart stalked up the path to give his report to the commandant.

11
The Hunt

As the days went on, it seemed to me that everyone except myself was proficient in the use of firearms. I cast about for some means of showing that I, too, could exhibit some dexterity in self-defense.

But what should the instrument be? I considered a bow and arrow, but discarded that thought. I would never be able to make the necessary arrows, and I knew that the Cherokee valued their supplies above everything.

One day, among the trade items, I noticed a small, nicely balanced hatchet. The Indians called such tomahawks. It was shaped like an axe, but was much smaller. Its iron head was bound upon the short handle with rawhide thongs that, being dried, bound it tightly. Perhaps this would be my weapon.

After my work was over for the day I set off by the river bank and, selecting an open space, set up a stake for a target and practiced throwing.

I was awkward. The tomahawk seldom came near the target. Laboriously, I trudged back and forth to retrieve my clumsy throws and sighed to think how long this would take. I extended my arm, preparing to make another throw, when a strong hand relieved me of it and then accurately tossed it, end over end, until it split the target.

Amazed, I turned. There at my elbow stood Tsalohi, my acquaintance of the trading path. His face was expressionless as usual, but there was a twinkle in his eye.

I laughed. "Tsalohi!" I greeted him. Then I pointed to myself, "Angus."

I hurried to the tomahawk and brought it to him and asked to be shown how he made such a throw. He comprehended my question and, stepping forward, cast the weapon again and hit the exact spot as before. I shook my head. I could not understand the accuracy of his seemingly unguided throw.

Tsalohi then showed me how to hold the weapon, and, with a quick turn of the wrist, he cast it end over end, the cutting edge hitting first. I was lost in admiration of such skill and shook my head over my own efforts.

It came about that when the day's work was done, Tsalohi would appear and tutor me in this new skill. I practiced faithfully, yet he was always the master.

One day Tsalohi appeared at Mistress Bacon's store and asked for me. I was sent for, and Mr. Shorey translated Tsalohi's request. He wished me to go on a deer hunt with him, and it would take us two days. Having got permission from Captain Demere, I followed my friend with a light heart.

He started out at a fast trot. I followed him easily. I had been swimming every day and had been on my feet from morning to night while carrying on my various duties about the fort. Consequently, my muscles had hardened since the days on the trading path.

Tsalohi's path took us through the villages south of the river. As we passed through one village after another, I began to see a pattern common to all. They were usually small—not over thirty houses—situated by the river. The houses clustered about an open central plaza. All were of the "overturned basket" architecture I had noticed in Chota; they were daubed with white clay on the outside and had roofs built of bark.

I was an object of curiosity whenever we appeared. Small boys followed me and with shrieks of laughter called attention to my red hair and white man's clothes. Tsalohi and I stalked through these small warriors with as much dignity as we could muster.

Our progress was considerably slower whenever we approached a group of girls. They smiled and whispered to one another as we passed. If a young Cherokee could be said to blush, I'm sure Tsalohi did, even though he gave a good appearance of indifference.

We came to Chota and the council house I had entered on the occasion of our ceremonial visit. Tsalohi led the way to his own home. Presiding here was a woman with a singular sweetness of face. I found out later that this was Tsalohi's aunt.

Tsalohi disappeared within the house and returned bearing a large quiver of arrows and a huge bow.

A slender girl, apparently Tsalohi's sister, came running and with animated gesture asked to go with us. Her aunt scolded, as did Tsalohi. Apparently, the girl was told that hunting was for men and that the housekeeping duties were her lot.

A stormy scene followed, in which the girl finally turned her back on her brother and, with a toss of her head, went into the house. Her defiant attitude promised trouble.

Tsalohi looked at me and shrugged, for all the world like Captain Demere, and we started on the hunt.

Again our progress was halted by a group of maidens calling and teasing as we walked through them. Suddenly Tsalohi came to an abrupt stop, his eyes on a girl carrying a large basket who had not taken part in the raillery of the others. He spoke in greeting, and she answered, eyes modestly downcast. Then the girl looked at me and smiled.

"Unaka." she said.

Tsalohi answered something that I took to be satisfactory, for she smiled and went on her way.

Our journey now began in earnest. Leaving the villages, we swam to the northside of the river. I was soon completely lost.

We encountered ridges, each rising higher than the other. Finally we came to one that overlooked the others. Below us lay a valley with a small stream wandering through a meadow. Here Tsalohi stretched himself on a large rock cresting the ridge, I beside him, and studied the valley.

A sound from the trail over which we had come disturbed us. Tsalohi retreated to a nearby tree. From this vantage point he peered down on our recent path.

Even in the afternoon sunlight his lithe form was so mottled by the shadows of the tree branches that he was indistinguishable from the bark. Almost before my eyes, my friend seemed to have vanished.

Apparently all was well, for he soon came to lie beside me. Now a herd of deer appeared in the little valley below us. Tsalohi rose and, lifting his face, began a low, impassioned chant. When it was ended, he beckoned me to follow.

We crept down the ridge to the right and came to the edge of the meadow. I realized that my companion had been constantly testing the direction of the wind. Upwind of us was the herd, guarded by a buck, his antlers carried high.

Tsalohi fitted an arrow to his bow and melted into the underbrush. I did not follow, fearing my clumsiness might alert the deer. When I next spied Tsalohi he was getting close to one of the does cropping the long grass at the edge of the meadow. The loud twang of his bowstring broke the silence. The doe sprang into the air and fell. The buck snorted, and the herd was gone in an instant.

Suddenly a triumphant voice was raised. Turning in alarm, we beheld a small figure on the rock where we had been lying. Tsalohi rose in wrath and motioned urgently. The figure scrambled down and out of sight. Then, reappearing, she came running toward us. It was Tsalohi's sister! Laughing and exultant, she stood above the fallen doe. She, too, had come on the hunt!

Exasperated beyond measure, Tsalohi seized the intruder. He urged me with an angry movement of his arm to follow. We fled into the shadows of the trees, where we crouched for all the world as if Creeks were at our heels. I was mystified. Why so angry, and why the desperate silence? We lay and watched the doe, half-hidden in the grass. Nothing stirred.

Then—an astonishing thing—the girl put her lips to my ear and whispered, "My brother is angry with me!"

I jerked my head about as if struck and stared at the small, mischievous face. Had I heard right? Apparently I had, for she added, still whispering, "He thinks hunting is only for men!"

There was an angry, whispered command from the affronted brother, and she was silent. Again we lay listening.

The tension in Tsalohi's alert body subsided. He sat up, regarding his sister with marked disfavor and addressed her briefly; then he arose and approached the fallen doe. We followed, and the new hunter said to me, "My brother says that if I am to be a hunter, I must do the hard work too!"

Cleaning the deer was hard work, and hot work, and before we were through our garments and limbs were blood-stained. Tsalohi directed our movements. After the carcass was disembowelled, he ripped off the hide. Every piece was destined for use, even the hoofs. Securing a strong tree branch, I was put to stripping it of bark and branches. By that time the meat had been roughly cut. The empty hide enfolded all the pieces, and then the heavy bundle was laced upon the pole by using some of the sinews of the deer. Carrying the pole across our shoulders, we made our way to the nearby stream.

Tsalohi had earlier cut out the tongue, and he cast a piece of it into the water. He watched as the blood was carried away. Then he leaped into the stream, dived into the water, and came up cleansed.

His good humor now restored, he sat on the bank while the two of us dived into the stream also, and I swam at some length. The girl clambered to where her brother sat and addressed him earnestly to such effect that when I came to rest beside them peace was restored.

In her curiously accented English she informed me, "My brother has forgiven me."

Tsalohi made an emphatic denial, and she added, "But he has not forgiven me for calling loud in the forest. That"—she searched for a word—"is absolutely forbidden! It is very dangerous!"

Pleased with this communication, she subsided into a smug demureness, as of a kitten that had gotten away with some small sin.

"I must learn to be a hunter and a warrior, because I will be a war-woman."

She saw my puzzled face and instructed me, "I will be very important. I will make the black drink and speak in council and wave a swan's wing."

I shook my head in bewilderment.

"Is not that the way of the *Unaka* women?" she asked.

97

"Unaka?"

"That is our word for 'white,'" she explained.

"No, I think not."

"Heh! They are not then important!"

The sun was lower. Tsalohi had now risen. Resuming our burden, we climbed to the rock where we had first sighted the deer.

Here we prepared to camp for the night. Strips of venison and the rest of the tongue were saved, and the deerskin, with its burden, was hung upon the limb of a tree. It was far enough from our encampment so as not to attract marauding animals to us.

Tsalohi now selected dead branches of a certain tree for his fire. The reason was soon apparent, for the fire burned without smoke. Before long a satisfactory bed of coals was ready.

He broke off several green branches and stripped them of leaves and bark. These he bound into a tripod on which were hung the strips of meat to roast. While the cooking was proceeding, he cut yet another piece of the tongue and flung it into the fire.

"That is for the Great Kanati" said my small teacher. "The other was for the river, for he is in the water and the fire."

We feasted royally that night. Tsalohi added grapes and chestnuts from his pouch.

After eating, we sat silently about the dying embers, looking toward the west, where the forest made a huge shadow against the still-light sky. The stars came out. Below us the river was a ribbon of light. The quiet was as deep as summer dust.

Tsalohi's curious chants kept ringing in my ears. His voice had had an intensity and passion that recalled my father's rapt intoning of the psalms.

"Little sister . . ." I began.

"I am not your sister. I am Ahwinita."

I started again. "Ahwinita, will you teach me . . .?"

"Oh, yes!" I was instantly forgiven.

"Teach me what your brother's hunting song says in my language?"

She sprang up, pleased to comply. Assuming in some odd way the very stance and reverent tone of Tsalohi, she lifted her eyes to the sky and said: "O Great Kanati, I come where you dwell. Let your bosom be covered with blood-stained leaves. And you, O Ancient Red, may you hover above my breast while I sleep. Let good dreams come. Let my hunting be good. Give me the wind, and let my paths be directed."

Instantly, she was a child again. She seated herself and continued: "There are four winds, you know. The south wind is white and brings peace. The west wind is black and brings death. The north wind is blue and brings trouble. But the east wind is red and brings war!"

It was very evident that she preferred the east wind!

"Where did you learn to speak . . . ?"

"As the *Unakas* do?"

"Yes."

"My brother and I were put in the home of Mr. Shorey when my mother died. I lived with them until my new mother could take me."

"How old are you?"

She spread her fingers out and counted proudly up to thirteen, her great age. She sighed, "I am very old. I shall be married very soon."

Tsalohi had been an interested listener to our conversation. His amusement was evident. His teasing voice addressed her at this statement.

She translated for me. "My brother says no warrior will

wife a woman who runs about the forest and is a great hunter."

Tsalohi stirred the fire and, covering the coals, admonished us to sleep.

I lay thinking of the hunting song and of the four winds.

There was a small whisper.

"What is your name?" Ahwinita asked.

"Angus."

"Heh! It is a hard name—An-gus!"

Early the next morning we broke camp and carried the deer meat to Tsalohi's home. One special delicacy, the rest of the tongue, was set aside and laid silently at the door of the young woman with the basket.

I thought myself an accomplished woodsman by this time and set out alone for the fort, bidding Tsalohi and his family a farewell.

12
Hostages

As the days passed, the gold and red of the forest sank to deep browns. The Indian corn in the fields to the east of the fort had long been harvested, the pumpkins and beans garnered. The noon sun was warm, but the nights were sharp.

Late one night I was brought sharply awake by the sound of galloping hoofbeats of an approaching horse in the distance; then there was a thunderous knocking at the eastern gate and a sharp challenge from the sentry. The big gates creaked on their hinges. Shortly a guard came running.

"Ferguson! Cap'n wants you! Come a'running!"

I trotted on his heels. Candles had been lit within the officers' quarters. The two captains were in their shirt-sleeves, facing the express rider who sat collapsed on a bench, his head in his hands.

Captain Demere busied himself opening the dispatches, then sat and read, lost in concentration.

Captain Stuart demanded of the rider: "Can you answer questions?"

"Oh, yes, sir!"

"Are you hungry?"

"Thirsty, mostly, sir."

The captain motioned to the sentry, and he sped out the door. He returned with a cup of water and a loaf of bread. The express drank the water at a gulp and then reached for the bread. His mouth full, he nodded to the captain that he was ready.

The captains had been giving close attention to the documents before them. They looked at each other, their faces guarded.

Captain Demere turned his attention to the rider. "Now, sir, if you will be so kind—a few questions."

"Yes, sir," said the messenger, wiping his mouth with his sleeve but keeping the bread handy.

"This document says that Governor Lyttelton has clapped twenty-eight chiefs and headmen into—whatever this means—'protective custody.' "

"Yes, sir—that means gaol."

"Where? Charles Town?"

"No, sir. Fort Prince George."

"At Fort Prince George?" Captain Stuart's surprised voice broke in.

"You see, sir, the governor marched with the army from Charles Town to Fort Prince George, and he took all them Cherokee chiefs along . . . "

"Yes, yes. We've read what it says," responded Captain Stuart testily.

The dark captain broke in wrathfully, "But why? No one tells me why!"

He whirled on the man, who cowered as if expecting a blow.

"Can you tell me?"

"All the governor was a'saying was to hold 'em hostage for the good behavior of the whole Cherokee nation."

At Captain Demere's shocked exclamation, he added, "If you're asking me, sir—and of course you don't have to consult my opinion, having all those documents there—I think the governor's got his wind up!"

Captain Demere laughed. "That is the first sensible word I have heard this night! Hostages, good God!"

Captain Stuart raised his eyes from the letter. "Demere, do you realize that one of the prisoners, or hostages—the difference escapes me—is Oconostota?"

"Oconostota?" echoed Demere in disbelief.

"The Great Warrior in custody? If the governor desired to insult the entire Cherokee nation, he could not have chosen better."

He turned to me. "Get Lieutenant Adamson immediately."

Captain Demere demanded of the lieutenant when he appeared, "Who's the rider who knows the trading path best?"

"That will be Huger, sir."

"Get him ready to ride by daylight. Select the best horse, too. We'll have the dispatches by that time."

"Yes, sir."

Captain Demere dismissed the messenger, then looked at me, as if he had suddenly recollected my presence.

"Well, Ferguson, there's much work to be done. Sit down, man, sit down and get on with it."

So began several hours' work for the three of us. The captains weighed alternatives, suggested and discarded plans of action, and when they were agreed, I began writing the letters. First, a letter to the governor, couching in polite phrases their suggestions that the chiefs and headmen be relieved from custody for the good of peaceful relations with the Cherokee.

"He won't accept that advice from us, Demere!"

"I know it," said the captain, "but someone has to say it."

Next, a letter was drafted to Attakullakulla, asking his understanding and good offices for a peaceful settlement to restrain the chiefs.

"Restrain!" snorted Captain Demere angrily.

I was sent to rouse Mr. Shorey. He appeared and was bidden to travel at daylight to Attakullakulla with the letter, and then to the lodging of Connecorte, the principal chief.

"Tell Attakullakulla I'll come myself if Connecorte wishes to see me," said Captain Stuart.

At the first light Huger and Mr. Storey came to the door and received the dispatches.

"If the governor has returned to Charles Town, follow him there," directed Captain Demere.

The captains and I watched the two riders pass through the gate, the candles guttering behind us on the table.

"And do you know, Stuart," mused Captain Demere, "the governor said when he returned to Charles Town he would proclaim a victory celebration?"

"I read it," said Captain Stuart. "I still don't believe it."

From that time on the tempo of activities about the fort quickened. Sentries were doubled at night, and the horses and cows in the north meadow were more closely guarded. Men were detailed for hunting and fishing; the game and fish brought in were salted and stored. Soldiers were sent out to fell trees and bring in the wood for fires. This was neatly stacked behind the barracks. The smithy and forges worked early and late, and hammers rang constantly.

The captains went over the tally of ammunition with Joseph Callaway, the gunner. A list was prepared to be ready for the next packtrain. Daily, express riders went down the trading path.

There was more than one route to Charles Town, and the captains were determined to learn them. Many nights were spent with runners and traders. Maps of the territory were drawn and perfected. Every hazard of the trading path was noted, every overhanging boulder or deep morass where danger might threaten was marked, for the Charles Town trading path was our lifeline, and on it depended our survival.

Fort Loudoun celebrated the king's birthday on a November day under leaden skies. Now the rains began in earnest. Supplies and clothing were soaked, as many soldiers as could kept within doors, and tempers were short. The parade ground was miry clay.

No Cherokees came to Mistress Bacon's store now, so the supplies were brought within and put away. I bedded down at night under the roof of the blacksmith's shop as near as I could get to the banked warmth of the forge.

An express came one day with the welcome news that Attakullakulla had visited Fort Prince George and had been partially successful. He had negotiated the release of Oconostota and three other chiefs, but twenty-four were still held.

The two captains continued to prowl the fort and the ramparts, inspecting every corner, every item. Day or night, they or the other officers were about when one least expected them. The guard dogs that had been kept by the soldiers who lived outside the fort were brought in and used on night patrol by the sentries.

It was fortunate that added precaution had been taken, for one night a clamor broke out in the north meadow where the cattle and horses were kept. Soldiers scrambled out the little postern gate set in that side of the wall. Those of us within could distinguish the screams and bawlings of horses and cattle, then mocking taunts of the attackers. Cherokees had broken into the stockade! When the frantic dogs were turned loose, the invaders disappeared as suddenly as they had come. It was a long time until quiet was restored.

The following morning the cattle and horses were

105

driven in and thereafter stabled within the fort. To the fort's military aspect were now added barnyard smells. The displeasure of the garrison was loud and derisive. Soldiers who declared they had taken the king's service only to escape the drudgery of farm life went about with fingers held to their noses.

Christmas came and went, marked only by a somber reading of the Scriptures. The soldiers spoke of a holiday dance at the fort when times had been more festive.

Nanye'hi came one day, bundled against the cold. She brought the news of Connecorte's death. Great mourning was being made for him, and he was to be buried with all appropriate ceremony. An old and valued friend of the British, he had held great power in the Cherokee nation. Who would succeed him as principal chief?

Soon the answer came: Kuhna-gatota was now principal chief of the nation, and his war chief was to be the Great Warrior, Oconostota, he who had been held an English prisoner!

One happy day a challenge rang out at the central gate. In came Mr. Elliot's packhorse train and, with it, Abram.

I heard his booming voice and ran to greet him. To my delight he delivered me a letter from Dr. DuPree. I tore open the paper and read that the good doctor was anxious about my safety—a concern "in which my daughter joins me." He had followed carefully the news of the fort, gained from traders and from members of the Assembly. Jamie was well and was being instructed in his letters. All was well on Meeting Street. I read this letter over many times; indeed, it was to become thin from much handling.

Abram and the drovers unloaded the new supplies. The ammunition was carried to the odd half-buried structure that I had noticed earlier. Here it was stored in tidy rows of barrels. Containers of sand stood just within the doors, ready in case of a spark, and a continuous guard was maintained. Foodstuffs, salt, and flour were stored under the lean-to sheds where the baking ovens stood. Blankets, uniforms, and boots were distributed.

Abram bedded down beside me that night and gave me news of the friends in Charles Town and of activities along the harbor. No further information had ever been obtained about my attackers.

The next express came one cold night. The soldier wearily climbed off his exhausted horse and announced that Cherokees had shot at him several times.

The message was that Oconostota and several warriors had appeared before the barred gates of Fort Prince George and demanded the release of the hostages. Lieutenant Coytmore, the commanding officer, had answered from within that until he received orders from the governor, he would not release the hostages.

Oconostota had then raised his voice and called to his friends within the gaol to keep up their spirits; he would return again. They had yelled answers to him, and he had left.

The two captains paced the room, much agitated, and sent for Lieutenant Adamson.

Captain Stuart gave his assessment of the situation. "Oconostota is an intelligent man and a determined one. He'll make good on his promise as soon as possible."

"What is your opinion, Adamson?" asked Captain Demere.

"I agree with Captain Stuart, sir. I fear, sir, that . . . " he hesitated.

"Yes?"

"Lieutenant Coytmore is very confident. He has contempt for the Indians as fighting men."

The dark captain remarked, "He should have been with General Braddock in '55. He would know better—if he had survived."

Captain Stuart was studying a sketch of Fort Prince George.

"Demere, he's safe, of course, as long as he stays within. With the swivel guns and the muskets he can hold off attackers for a long siege, until relieved."

"The danger is that he might be tempted outside . . . "

The three men sat and looked at the sketch without speaking. Finally the lieutenant remarked, "I'm glad I'm not in Coytmore's boots."

Captain Demere stared at him. "Did it occur to you, Lieutenant, that this fort is in exactly the predicament of Fort Prince George?"

The lieutenant's ears reddened. "No, sir, I had not thought of that."

"You might also reflect upon the fact that we are some one hundred miles farther from any source of help!"

So a letter was drafted to Lieutenant Coytmore at Fort Prince George.

Sir: We are certain that Oconostota plans to strike the war pole very soon. We are also sure that you are ready for any eventuality; however, we should warn you against any stratagem of peace or parley on the part of the Cherokees. We are sending on this intelligence to Governor Lyttelton, but wished to warn you also.

Demere

I was directed to copy this for delivery to Charles Town also.

108

"Who is the next express rider?" asked Captain Demere.

"McLemore, sir. I'll fetch him." And Lieutenant Adamson left.

"When can you be ready to ride, sir?" Captain Demere asked the rider when he arrived.

He stood twisting his hat in his hand.

"I been talking to the last man, sir."

The captain raised an astonished face. "This is no answer to my question."

The man shifted from one foot to the other, miserably ill at ease.

"I'm trying to explain, sir."

"Explain!"

"You see the last rider was shot at . . . "

"So he informed me."

"And he says the Cherokees can hear a horse going down that path a mile away. He says as how it's certain death for any express to get through."

"I am not interested in his opinion, sir. I asked when you can ride!"

The man wiped the sweat from his face.

"Captain, you can order me to go down that path, and I'll have to go or else stand a court-martial. But I hope you won't ask it, sir!"

The man hurried on. "I'm trying to explain, sir. I don't so much mind being shot, but I've seen what can happen to a man taken alive. Torture ain't something I'd wish for, Captain. Now, a good woodsman, sir—which I ain't and never was—traveling on foot stands a good chance to get through. But a man on horseback ain't got a prayer."

I doubt that the man had ever made a longer speech or one more affecting to his hearers, for Captain Demere's

109

voice was kind. "Very well, McLemore. You've put your case very well. You may go."

A look of intense relief came over the man's face, and he left quietly.

"There are limits to one's powers to command, are there not?" sighed the captain.

"Now"—he turned his attention to Captain Stuart— "who is our best woodsman?"

I was startled by the recollection of something faintly remembered.

"Come, come, Angus," said Captain Stuart. "Have you thought of someone?"

"Yes, sir," I answered hesitantly. "Something Abram said to me once . . . "

"Yes?" he prompted.

"He said he'd traveled the trading path so often he could follow it with his eyes shut."

"Abram!" said Captain Stuart. "Why didn't we think of him?"

Captain Demere spoke up. "For a very good reason, Stuart. His Majesty's officers may command a soldier, but they may not command a slave. He belongs to Samuel Benn.

"We cannot command him," he concluded, "but to offer him an amount commensurate with the service— would that not be possible?"

A great thought struck me, and I dared to break in. "Please don't offer him money, Captain. He's a proud man, as proud as any Cherokee chief! Offer him his freedom!"

Pleased smiles broke out on the captains' faces, and it was a great pleasure to hear Captain Stuart's comment: "An old head on young shoulders, Angus."

So Abram was summoned, and the offer explained. He

110

stood tall, and his eyes glowed as though candles were lighted in his head.

"Thank you kindly, Cap'n. I accepts."

"And if the governor chooses not to honor our agreement, sir," stated Captain Demere. "I shall be personally responsible for the reward."

"Don't give me no letter, Cap'n. It might get lost. I remember it. If'n I don't get through, de letter lost anyway."

The letter was read to him, and he repeated the contents word for word.

The next hour was spent in going over the route he had so often taken. Every admonition and caution that the officers had been able to gather in the past months was added to his knowledge of the path. Our hopes rose.

"Now, gentlemens," Abram concluded, "I'd better start now." He laughed. "Me—I kin to owls—I see in de dark."

I was sent to fetch a small bag of jerky and dried corn—Abram said if it was good enough for the Indians, it was good enough for him—and the candles were doused. We stepped out into the darkness.

Captain Stuart led the way to the river gate—that pathway being most likely to be unobserved.

"Wait, Abram," I whispered. I could not let him go without telling him how much I owed him, but when I stared up into his kind face the fine words deserted me. Captain Stuart spoke to the sentry at the gate. We shook Abram's hand, and then the darkness swallowed up the tall figure.

When I lay down in my accustomed place, sleep was a long time in coming. I breathed a sincere prayer for his safety—and our own.

111

13
The Messengers

One day in February as I was helping in the captains' office, the sentry knocked on the door and Nanye'hi was admitted. In her hands was a large basket that she presented to Captain Demere.

"Nuts and dried grapes for the captains' table from Attakullakulla," she said. "He sends a message also."

After one flashing glance around the room that took in everything, the Cherokee woman stood immobile. The two captains rose to their feet.

"Thank you, madame. Pray be seated."

She seated herself composedly.

"What is Chief Attakullakulla's message?"

"Tomorrow the warriors will drink the black drink."

"The black drink!" the captains exclaimed.

"Where do the warriors go?" asked Captain Demere.

"Where? To Fort Prince George, naturally."

The captains looked at each other.

"How many go?"

"A sufficient number, my captains, to free the hostages held there."

"Who leads them?"

"Oconostota. He has sworn an oath that he will not come back without the hostages. As you know, my captains, no ambassador of our people has ever been taken hostage, as these chiefs were when they went in peace at the invitation of your governor. You, yourself, Captain Stuart, took the invitation to the council house at Chota."

Captain Stuart responded sadly, "I did, indeed, and I assure you it was in good faith on my part."

Captain Demere spoke bitterly, "We are not informed here in Fort Loudoun what is in the royal governor's mind in Charles Town."

Nanye'hi arose, drawing her shawl about her. The captains stood.

"Madame," said Captain Demere, "we are greatly in your debt for this information, as well as for the gift from the great Chief Attakullakulla. May I ask of you one question?"

She nodded silently.

"Why do you help us in our difficulties? Very few of your people are now our friends."

When she answered, her low voice was charged with deep emotion. "When the red wind of war blows upon my people, we perish."

Captain Stuart inquired, "Are you not afraid to come to us?"

She laughed. "My death would be avenged."

She left and passed out of the gates the sentry opened for her, unhurried and unafraid.

My curiosity got the better of me.

"What does she mean by 'the black drink'?"

"The black drink is a ceremonial drink, Angus—a strong purgative made from the yaupon holly." Captain Stuart answered. "Its purpose is to cleanse the body. One of the times when it is used is preparation for the warpath."

When my work was done, I prowled the confines of the fort. I climbed upon the bastion next to the river and sat, sunk in my gloomy thoughts. The thought of painted warriors stealing upon the small fort to the south was a disturbing one. If the Cherokee warriors should take Fort

Prince George, what was there to keep them from attacking Fort Loudoun?

From my perch I stared at the bare, stripped trees on the heights opposite the fort. Below ran the cold sparkle of the river. Suddenly I saw Tsalohi, the shadows of the forest concealing him to any but the keenest eye. He did not move, only stood looking at me. The sharpest longing struck me. What did it matter that a royal governor had done a stupid thing? What did it matter that Oconostota was on the warpath? Tsalohi and I were friends, and I was eager to tell him so.

I glanced about. The sentry on the bastion was at the farthest corner; below, the sentry at the river gate was also preoccupied with his duties. I slipped down from my perch and sought out Mistress Bacon. She was occupied mending garments.

"Ain't seen you lately," she said. "You helping the captains run this place?"

"Yes, ma'am. It's harder work than any I ever did for you."

"What you want, boy?"

"Haven't you a good knife in the trade goods, Mistress Bacon?"

"A fine one."

She searched the boxes and handed me a long knife that the hunters among the soldiers were fond of.

"Then I'd like a hawkbell."

"What you going to do with such a play-pretty?" she asked suspiciously.

"Might find me a hawk, ma'am."

Requesting her to charge those items to my account, I added a fishing cane and line.

"You ain't a'going into them woods, my boy!" she admonished.

114

I shrugged and said nothing.

Shortly afterwards, I wandered down by the river gate and struck up a conversation with the bored sentry. He eyed the fishing pole alertly, however.

"There's mighty good fishing right outside that gate, corporal," I said.

"Don't I know it. I can smell 'em!" He glared at me. "But all soldiers is confined to the fort."

"But I'm not a soldier."

He frowned. "So you're not, Ferguson."

"If you let me out that gate, sort of quietlike, I'll share my catch with you."

"You get in trouble," he warned, "and the captains will know who let you out."

"Trouble? It's daylight, corporal."

"Well," he looked about, "out you go, and mind you, come back afore I'm off duty."

I slipped through and was free. There was no movement across the river. I walked downstream until a thicket of small trees hid me from the bastion above. Continuing still farther, I found a satisfactory spot and was soon fishing. If Tsalohi had seen me, I was sure he would come.

Before many minutes had passed, a dark head broke the surface. Tsalohi climbed out, shook himself as a dog does, and sat beside me. He looked at me. I could not tell if he were pleased. Suddenly, his eyes sparkled.

Drawing out the new knife, I placed the shaft of it in his hand and gestured that it was his. Then I added the hawkbell and indicated that it was for Ahwinita.

Trying out my few phrases of his language, I came out very hesitantly with *tso-ga-li-i,* which Mr. Shorey had assured me meant "friends."

A startled expression crossed his face, and, for the first

115

time since I had met him, Tsalohi broke into a laugh. He set about to correct my pronunciation—thus, and thus only!—and the Cherokee word for "friends" came out of his mouth a vastly different word from the hesitant syllables I had spoken.

The rest of the hour was spent silently fishing. He helped me pull several sizeable fish out of the river, using my pole in a fashion obviously laborious for him. When at last I arose, he courteously declined my offer of his share of our catch. He slipped silently into the river and was lost to sight.

I tapped on the river gate and was admitted by a relieved sentry. He whispered his thanks and hid his two fish under his woolen matchcoat.

Mistress Bacon cooked my fish for me, and we feasted. She said never a word about where it came from.

Mr. Shorey would disappear for days at a time, only to reappear without explanation. He came and went, accountable to no one but the captains. So it was not remarked when he entered by the river gate one cold day at dusk and knocked for admittance at the officers' quarters.

"Message for you, Cap'n Demere," he announced.

"Come in, Shorey," said Captain Stuart. We had been laboring longer than usual over the tally of foodstuffs, since the captains were anxious to keep a four-months' supply ahead.

"Begging your pardon, sir," said Mr. Shorey. "You are both asked to the river gate. No lights. Special messenger sent by Attakullakulla."

Since I was a member of the captains' staff, although in a rather odd capacity, I followed closely, curious as to the unusual precautions.

116

Arriving at the river gate, Mr. Shorey begged that the sentry be withdrawn to a little distance. This request was complied with, and in the increasing darkness Mr. Shorey peered out the river gate and motioned to someone without.

We were greatly surprised when the slight figure of Ahwinita appeared. She backed against the gate, half-hiding behind Mr. Shorey. Her gaze swept the half-circle facing her and came to rest on my face. She dropped her eyes.

Mr. Shorey knelt and spoke to her gently in Cherokee. Then he explained to the captains, "This is Ahwinita. She came to my wife and asked to see you both. She is of Attakullakulla's family, and I've no doubt was selected as messenger for a good reason."

"What reason?" demanded Captain Demere.

"I don't know, sir."

"Tell her not to be afraid. We won't harm her."

Mr. Shorey translated. Her soft answer was in Cherokee. The short recital was received with startled exclamation from Mr. Shorey, who turned quickly to the officers.

"She says the Cherokees have surrounded Fort Prince George and Lieutenant Coytmore's been killed and all the hostages as well!"

"When?"

"As near as I can make out, three days ago."

Mr. Shorey asked question after question, then interpreted for the officers.

"Oconostota asked for a parley with Coytmore, and when the lieutenant came outside . . . "

"The fool—the fool!"

"He signaled warriors at a distance, and they shot the lieutenant and attacked the fort."

117

"But the hostages?" inquired Captain Stuart.

Another question, and then: "The garrison killed them all when Coytmore was shot."

"All?"

Another question. "Twenty-four, sir. No one got into the fort. The Cherokees have come home. All the villages are in mourning."

Captain Demere whirled on the girl. "Why did *she* bring the message? Why not a man?"

Ahwinita shrank back startled.

Another question. "She says the warriors are too angry. They will not speak in peace to a white man."

Mr. Shorey bent again to the girl. He looked at me. "Captain Demere, she has a message for Angus, alone."

"Certainly. Thank her for the message, and if she wants anything . . . " His voice trailed off.

Mr. Shorey's voice was courteous. "She will take nothing."

The two captains moved away.

I knelt before Ahwinita. She gave her message to Mr. Shorey, gazing at me steadily the while.

"Listen carefully: the message is from Tsalohi."

I knew what the message would be. "Yes?"

"He is your friend no longer. The knife you gave in friendship, when next he sees you, will be raised against you in battle."

I looked into the dark eyes. "I want to give her a message in my own words, Mr. Shorey."

"Very well." Mr. Shorey moved aside.

"Ahwinita, tell your brother that I understand. Some-day, when you are a war-woman, remember me."

Large tears gathered in her eyes. She extended a hand to me, gently placed the hawkbell in my hand, and was gone.

118

14
The Siege

From that time on, preparations for an attack were perfected—for all knew an attack was coming.

Cherokee wives elected to go back to their people, taking their children with them. We watched them as they left, trudging down the path to the farther villages, bundles on their arms and small dark heads bobbing in the cradleboards on their backs. The larger children ran beside them, turning occasionally to wave to their fathers on the bastions.

The remaining families were brought inside the fort. Men moved out of the barracks in order to give the women and children room and made shift themselves to sleep under various shelters.

The wives, being experienced campaigners, set to and gave their husbands and the garrison a great deal of encouragement by their cheerful assumption of chores. Men became more spruce in their dress and more agreeable in their manners. An odd sort of gaiety settled in.

The greening woods changed daily. The river rose after the fresh rains. Frogs of all voices made an ever-swelling chorus in the meadows, and the birds appeared, often in large, noisy flocks.

Ammunition for the cannons was carried to the bastions and covered against the weather. Each man was assigned a certain station, and those who did not handle guns or serve the cannon were drilled in fetching water and sand to extinguish possible fires.

Bread enough for days ahead was baked and stored. The smithy rang incessantly with the job of getting all guns repaired and items of metal and harnesses put in order.

I had not known there were two medical men at the fort, having noticed only Lieutenant Maurice Anderson, a bluff, red-faced man who seemed more fond of hunting than of the practice of medicine. He took it as a personal affront that the Cherokees had interfered with his frequent hunting trips. The surgeon's mate was John Johnston, a thin, broken reed of a man who seemed very fond of the bottle. I never knew his source of supply, for the captains were adamant in refusing rum to the men. I suppose the traders supplied him.

The Cherokee wives still visited the fort, and from them we learned that Attakullakulla stood alone. All it wanted, it seemed, was the day of the attack.

Finally, it came. In the darkness of an early March morning, there was a crescendo of yells and shots. Drumbeats called us to our stations, and we ran to our places. We peered through the half-darkness and fog to see, just out of range, the tall figure of Kahna-gatota lift his arm and signal to warriors half-concealed in the edge of the forest. For a moment we stared at the painted figures, and then they disappeared in the smoke of the incessant firing—our guns and theirs.

The cannons were brought into play. Derisive laughter and singing greeted the cannon blasts, and an occasional tree came crashing down, but that was the only visible effect.

Food and water were carried to the men on the bastions and at the firing stations. They ate where they stood and slept not at all.

An incautious soldier rising to aim more carefully would

be sought out by a spiteful bullet. A yell, a heavy fall from his station, and another man would take his place, more cautious this time. Most of the casualties were from splinters flying from the palisades. Blazing arrows came soaring into the fort, occasionally igniting the shingles of the barracks, but these fires were speedily extinguished.

Three days later came a deafening silence as the guns ceased. Soldiers fell asleep at their posts, exhausted by the strain.

Nothing moved in the forest. The officers prowled the perimeter, watching carefully. An occasional yell or taunt was raised, but that was all. And yet none ventured or were permitted to venture beyond the palisades, for outside, death waited patiently.

The garrison came to life again slowly, as if drugged. The doctor and the surgeon's mate circulated among the men, binding wounds and burns hitherto gone unnoticed. The cooking pots were filled with savory stews that the men ate in relays.

Although the firing had stopped, we were still surrounded by the Cherokees who permitted none of us to leave safely.

The carpenters inspected the defenses and repaired damage done by the burning arrows. The cattle within the fort were slaughtered and the meat salted down. That permitted a little more forage for the horses, but the supply diminished at an alarming rate.

In the following weeks curious things happened—boredom set in, tempers flared, men who had taken orders briskly began to lag and grow careless in their duties. Clothing wore out and was patched and patched again.

As summer came the cooking fires grew smaller, for the

ration of corn had been cut. The supply of wood, which had bulked so large at first, could not be replenished.

It was an effort to raise the water from the well. Now we went unwashed. Water was too precious for any use but for drinking and to be held against the threat of fire. When sudden, drenching downpours came, the women put out tubs and basins for washing. At such times particular care was necessary to keep the ammunition dry. The older men became more cheerful and opined that the Cherokees were in the same difficulty. Their officers reminded them tartly that their adversaries had an advantage in wet weather—arrows.

We began to look like scarecrows for lack of sleep, walking about dazed and half-aware. Even sleep did not refresh us. When we woke there were the same confining palisades, the parade ground either dusty and hot or a quagmire when it rained. The pitiful whining of the children, hungry and listless, irritated even the kindest of the soldiers.

We waited for relief, and none came.

Then, a shocking event occured: Luke Kraft defied an order. I suppose one would call it mutiny.

One day there was the roll call as usual with the men lined up in the hot sunshine to be assigned their duties for the day. It was a routine scene and probably a routine order given; no one remembered later what started the defiance. A loud, angry voice was suddenly raised in protest, and an angry private, young Kraft, confronted the sergeant.

"No, I will not!" he shouted, his red face within inches of the sergeant's startled visage.

There was a rush toward the rigid line of soldiers to hear what the ruckus was all about. I stood in the doorway of the officers' quarters and had an unobstructed view. I was thunderstruck and so, I guessed, was the sergeant.

Captain Demere came to stand beside me. "What is happening?" he asked.

I gestured toward the scene, speechless.

He glanced in that direction, then leaped down the steps and strode to confront the two antagonists. He seldom raised his voice, but I could hear him, and his tone was such as made my hair rise.

"Sergeant, what means this scene?"

Luke Kraft shouldered aside the paralyzed sergeant and flung his musket to the ground.

"I'll tell you what it's all about, Captain! I'm tired and hungry, and I ain't going to take no orders no more! It's do this and do that, and what's the good of it? Them Cherokees is just outside the fort, and we'll all be killed. I can't put up with it no more!"

He put up his hands to his face and bawled like a child.

Captain Demere's voice rang out. "Private Kraft, pick up your gun!"

Still sobbing, the private did so.

"Now, sir, follow me!" He turned to the sergeant. "Dismiss the men, sir!"

Captain Demere strode back to the officers' quarters, Kraft following meekly, and the door closed upon the two of them.

No one ever knew what was said and no one dared stay around to hear, but if a whole garrison could be said to go about on tiptoe, it did that day.

That night orders were read to the effect that Private Kraft had been assigned special duties as orderly to Captain Demere. After that, young Kraft walked about with a closed and belligerent air and said nothing to anybody.

The officers of the fort were the only ones I had ever seen, and one would not call them friendly or even less than correct. I suppose if there were a word to describe them it would be haughty. They were educated, professional men, and the rank and file were not. The noncommissioned officers were as proud and competent as their superiors. But some of the men were trouble-makers on sea or land. A few had been impressed by recruiters—kidnapped would be a more exact term—and only kept to rigid discipline by the threat of flogging or hanging. The king's pay and the king's food were all they lived for, and when their lives became unbearable they deserted.

But now desertion was not to be thought of. Between hanging or the death waiting in the silent woods, any sensible man would choose hanging.

The two captains began to make the rounds of the fort more frequently. There were no dispatches arriving or leaving to confine them to the cabin that served as their office.

One of the rounds was made just at early dusk when cooking pots were swung over the small fires. Spruce and immaculate as always, although their garments hung loosely on their persons, the two captains made the rounds, inspecting carefully.

Captain Stuart checked into the contents of one pot. Its attendant spoke. "I could make it a mite tastier, Cap'n, if I could run me down a squirrel to add to the corn and salt meat."

The captain laughed. "The next time I catch sight of Oconostota, I'll arrange a truce for you to do so."

Laughter broke out, and the remark was repeated again and again. We could follow its path around the campfires by the sudden shouts of laughter that made the circle.

The two captains stood listening, forgetting my presence.

Captain Stuart murmured, "I was not aware that I was so witty, Demere."

"Perhaps that is what we all need," mused the dark captain, "to think beyond this moment—to laugh—to hope."

Captain Stuart stared. "You have no hope?"

His companion looked at him. "For you, perhaps; for myself, none."

"None!"

"Be reasonable, Stuart! If you were Oconostota, with the deaths of twenty-four of your men to avenge, would you permit the commanding officer of your enemy to go free?"

"We should all pray for a speedy relief," Captain Stuart said.

"Do so," the captain answered and continued on his rounds.

My throat was dry. Icy fingers twisted my heart in my chest. I turned and fled—away from the laughter, away from the cooking fires. I was brought up short by the challenge of a sentry in the half-darkness. He loomed above me, peering down from his post on the bastion above. Was he afraid too?

I blundered into the palisade and sat huddled against it for comfort. How could the captain go on, talking, giving orders, making reports if he knew—? There came to my mind all the whispered tales the soldiers had told of how a man could be tortured by Indians.

I flung myself on the ground and found that I was blubbering as much as Luke Kraft ever did. I stifled my sobs so that the sentry would not hear. I must have dropped off to sleep, for I wakened later and decided to bed down there for the rest of the night.

The Cherokee wives still occasionally brought corn and vegetables to sell. They came with defiant, backward looks; calls and shouts from angry warriors pursued them. Once when Mr. Shorey came to help them with the baskets, they chattered away to him, with flashing eyes and saucy gestures. He burst into laughter and explained the situation to the many curious who flocked to hear: "These women have informed the braves that they still insist on supplying their husbands. They have been threatened with death, but their answer is that their relatives must avenge them, so they know very well that the warriors won't touch them." Everyone thought it a huge joke on our besiegers, and the visitors were twice welcomed—for food and for laughter.

That night about the supper fires, Mr. Shorey, that hitherto moody and reserved man, gave an impromptu dance, pantomiming the defiant wives, and the drummer boy entered into the spirit of things and beat the accompaniment. The soldiers sat in a circle and beat time and noisily applauded each hilarious episode. The officers stood in the background and laughed as heartily as the lowest private.

From that time on, it was taken for granted that entertainment of some kind be offered about the supper fires. If it were not offered willingly, the audience demanded it noisily. Mistress Bacon sang the interminable verses of "Barbara Allen." Then one night a shout was put up for "Angus—Angus Ferguson." I was plunked bodily into the center of the firelit circle and stood uncertainly. "Sing 'The Gypsy Lad,'" yelled Captain Stuart.

So I filled my lungs and gave them "The Gypsy Lad." Suddenly, Captain Stuart threw off his hat and coat, snatched a shawl from Mistress Bacon's shoulders, and, draping it about himself in the manner of a plaid, started a Highland fling. "Come on, Angus!" he yelled, "for the honor of Scotland!" And we gave a frantic—often stumbling—sword dance, wildly cheered by the assembled company.

Mistress Bacon laughed until she cried and declared it was the best dancing she'd ever seen. The captain and I looked at each other, sweating and grinning, and I was never before so proud of being a Scotsman.

Then a shout was put up for Captain Demere, but he declined, saying that one officer making a fool of himself at a time was enough, else where would be the discipline of His Majesty's army?

For days afterward I was congratulated as if I had been a hero, and "The Gypsy Lad" was sung and whistled on every side.

One night late in May the sentry's challenge rang out, and someone answered outside the river gate. Two men slipped inside. Instantly the whole fort came to life. Soldiers came running with torches, and in their light we saw a soldier and my friend Abram; the men were thin and weary, but quite pleased with themselves. They began to do a strange dance, divesting themselves of what few rags hung on them. Underneath, they were wound about with ribbons and braid! Producing small pots from about their persons, they added them to the small store—paint, of all things, and ribbons to be exchanged for food!

I rushed to see my friend and was greeted by a great hug.

"Boy, Abram a free man! Shout it! Lord God Almighty!"

He was jubilant. The Assembly of South Carolina had bought his freedom and granted him the great sum of £500 for "services rendered the state."

The two men had come from Fort Prince George, Abram having arrived from Charles Town, and brought wonderful news—a relief force was on the way! A force of twelve hundred men under Colonel Archibald Montgomery had landed in Charles Town early in April. They had been joined by over four hundred colonial troops and sympathetic Indians, and their objective was Fort Prince George and eventually Fort Loudoun. Colonel Montgomery's orders were to chastise the Cherokees, burn their towns, and relieve the two forts. We yelled ourselves hoarse. Help was on its way!

Abram and I sat apart for the remainder of the night. He recited the events of his short stay in the city. I fairly ached to hear. He told me how Savannah did and passed on the kind messages she sent. Dr. DuPree expressed a wish for my speedy return and suggested that I become his pupil in the study of medicine. Such a course seemed the happiest I'd ever conceived of, and I went about in a rosy glow, seeing myself in Charles Town, surrounded by friends, affection, peace—and, of course, plenty to eat!

Abram's feet were badly cut and lacerated in his recent travelings. Dr. Anderson and Mr. Johnston came to tend the wounds. Because other remedies were lacking, Abram's feet were soaked in hot water in which a little salt was dissolved, and then warm cloths were wrapped about them. By this time he could not walk, but sat in the shade of the blacksmith's shop, cheerily conversing with all and sundry.

In spite of the revived hope of rescue, there was

another cut in our rations. Now we were restricted to a little more than a cup of corn a day.

Hunger is a curious thing. One can say, "I will not think of food," but that is the sole thought one has. Our whole conversation centered on food—on how delicious a meal of squirrel stew would be, on how best to cook venison. We would describe in detail the special dishes of our childhood.

One day an old Cherokee woman came to the fort. She explained to Mr. Shorey that the *Unaka's* army was marching to the Middle Cherokee towns and many warriors had gone to fight them. Many we knew were still in the woods about us. She had a message that she would deliver alone to the "dark captain." After leaving the officers' quarters, she hurried out the river gate shaking her head at the offer of a length of bright ribbon.

Captain Demere called for me. The captain was sunk in a brown study when I arrived and failed to answer my greeting. Finally, he began to dictate, and I wrote as he spoke:

Fort Loudoun   May 10, 1760

Sir: Today I have this intelligence delivered to me from the chief Attakullakulla: A surprise attack against this fort is expected. He has attended every conference at the council house and had hoped to give me warning, but he believes now that the war party will not tell him their real thoughts, nor can he hope for more intelligence. He is taking his family and is retiring to the woods. He hopes to send me warning should he learn of any further plans. I have the honor to be,
Your excellency,

Paul Demere, Captain

The letter stayed on his desk. There was none to deliver it.

That night the officers made their rounds. If more time than usual was spent on the bastions, no one noticed it. The small fires were now very few, and the soldiers who were off duty lingered until the warm dusk settled down.

The officers halted in the flickering light. Captain Demere looked about and spoke, smiling. "You are now reduced to hear my performance tonight, my friends."

A cheer went up, and others came running and seated themselves in the circle.

"I shall sing you a little song I remember from my childhood," the captain said and raising his voice sang in a surprisingly sweet voice.

As the strains died away, someone asked, "I heard tell as how you fought with Braddock at that there river in Pennsylvania?"

"The Monongahela."

"Doggone! I can't never pronounce them Indian names! They say that Braddock was a coward."

"I was there, and I assure you, sir, he was most brave. Would one speak of a coward who climbs on four horses, each to be killed in turn, and then climbs on the fifth to meet his death? I think not."

"Captain, what did you do in that battle?" The question came from Mistress Bacon.

The captain turned toward her and smiled. "Ah, Madame Bacon, you embarrass me. A soldier is only remembered for his victories, never his defeats! And now, if you will permit, madame, I take my leave."

And he was gone.

I bedded down by Abram's improvised quarters that night, inquiring how he did. He assured me he was doing well. As we settled down to quietness, he whispered, "De dark captain—he brave man."

"How do you know, Abram?"

"Brave men don't never tell how brave they is—only how brave some other fella be."

The second day of June began with a happy event but ended in tragedy. For days, vague rumors disturbed the peace of the garrison. The Cherokee wives were now prevented by the warriors from bringing any food. Occasionally, one came and went empty-handed, furtive and preoccupied, instead of being talkative and cheerful as before. What was happening?

The sentries were not the only ones who stared out into the surrounding silence; theirs were not the only ears attuned to the sounds of the night. The garrison became restless and uneasy. We felt as men do when a storm approaches before there is a sign of a cloud or wind. We waited.

That morning the sudden alertness of the sentries on the southern bastion was immediately noticed. All who could, scrambled to the parapet there and saw three Cherokees approaching. First came Attakullakulla, an erect figure, dressed in breechclout and leggings, a single feather in his roach of hair. Following came two women, one quite elderly.

"Attakullakulla!" exclaimed the sentry, and someone ran to call the captain. The rest of us stayed glued to the parapet. The two captains, pulling on their jackets and clapping their hats on, hurried to the eastern gate and ordered it opened. They stood in the doorway to welcome their distinguished guest who advanced with unhurried step.

Captain Demere swept off his hat and bowed. "Welcome, my friend," he said.

131

The chief stood as proudly as if a whole battalion of warriors were at his back. He bowed his head in acknowledgment. King George himself could not have appeared more composed and regal in his bearing than our guest.

Captain Stuart rapped out an order, and a guard formed hastily. Respectfully surrounding Attakullakulla, the guard led to seats within the blacksmith shop, that being the only place shaded enough for the visit that now went forward with all due ceremony.

Food was produced from somewhere, a fire was started, and the kettle hung. In the shortest time possible, the food was cooked and presented to the guests. An occasional sentence was spoken, but the simple meal was served and eaten in silence.

Captain Demere brought out a clay pipe and, lighting the tobacco, offered it first to Attakullakulla who blew the smoke to the four points of the compass. The pipe passed back and forth among the officers. All then sat in deep meditation.

Captain Demere arose and made a speech of welcome, having Mr. Shorey by for the translation. It was then Attakullakulla's turn, and as he rose, all activity in the fort came to a halt and a silent ring of soldiers surrounded the officers and their guests. Pausing often so that his speech would have sufficient time for translation, he spoke:

"My friends, my family and I have come from our place in the forest to tell you again that the belt of friendship is unbroken between us. My people have struck the war pole, but that I shall never do. Long years ago the king across the water gave me this"—he dramatically raised a small silver medal on his breast—"and I gave a promise of friendship to him. There are many difficulties between my brother the white man and us his red brother, but we travel the same road. May it be in peace."

Captain Demere arose and invited the chief to his quarters, and the two captains and the chief went within. The door was closed and remained so for some time. Meanwhile Lieutenant Adamson busied himself arranging the impromptu honor guard, and when the door opened again, Attakullakulla was greeted by the reasonably military appearance of the guard. He and his family walked silently between the ranks, and the gate closed behind them.

Late in the afternoon of that same day, as the shadows from the great trees to the west were stealing across the ramparts, sudden yells and screams broke out beneath those trees. Men scrambled to the parapets. There we saw a horrifying sight. Out of range of our muskets a group of Cherokees was clustered about two men on the ground who were putting up a desperate but losing fight.

"It's the doctor and Swenson!" yelled someone. Fifty men promptly grabbed their guns and went racing out the nearest gate to the rescue to be met by a hot fire from Cherokees yet concealed.

The two captains came running, yelling at the soldiers to return. By that time the two men they had attempted to rescue were still, and soon two awful, bloody scalps were raised high in triumph. Amid yells of victory the attackers faded into the forest.

Shocked and in broken ranks, the men straggled back and the gate was barred. For a long time yells of triumph and scattered shots came from unseen antagonists. The two silent figures lay in full view, and those watching wept with rage and helplessness.

The returned soldiers slumped to the ground, cursing. Several men were wounded, and Mr. Johnston, the surgeon's mate, and Mistress Bacon moved among them. Captain Demere confronted the men in a towering rage.

"Who gave the order to open that gate?" he demanded. No one answered. It finally came out that dozens of hands had opened it.

"You fools!" cried the captain. "The only reason the Cherokees didn't come pouring in was because they were too busy with the two outside. Why were they out there? Does anyone know?"

Luke Kraft spoke up. "I heard Anderson and Swenson talking last night, Captain, saying as how they were going hunting the first chance they got. I reckon they figured it had been quiet so long there weren't no Indians about."

"That's just what they wanted you to think. Well, the doctor and Swenson are done for. I won't risk another attack by allowing any of you to bury them now. A detail will go only when I give the order. Have you forgotten so soon what happened at Prince George! It shall not happen here!"

That night the captain picked a detachment of expert marksmen who slipped out of the fort to surround the slain men. They stood guard while others buried them where they fell.

Prayers for the dead were offered when the grim business was concluded, and a double watch was set. The remainder of the night was quiet. The men were restless, however, and an air of angry hopelessness pervaded the camp.

15
Through Peril

The question from then on was, Where is Montgomery and his army? Several days later we were given a partial answer. A soldier from Prince George, his clothes in tatters, slipped into our fort. Captain Demere heard him out in front of the whole garrison. The man said Montgomery and his army had arrived at Fort Prince George early in June and were preparing to march to the Lower towns to chastise the Cherokees and burn their homes. Then he would proceed to the Middle and Overhill towns and eventually to Fort Loudoun.

A stunned silence greeted this news. Suddenly a gaunt, lean figure sprang to confront the captain.

"Lord God Almighty, Captain," he protested. "Send word to that there general to hurry, or we'll all be dead men and ghosts afore he gets here! He's got over fifteen hundred men! If I had half that number of Carolina men and a little food, we'd be halfway to Charles Town!"

An angry yell from the assembled hearers spoke eloquently of like opinions.

The dark captain raised his hand for silence. It was given grudgingly. His glance swept around the company. "Mr. Mouncey, my orders are to hold this fort until relieved, and I shall do so." A sudden smile touched his severe features, and he added, "Should God grant me the number of Carolinians that you mention, I would be the first to give the order to march!"

A startled laugh began and spread. The tension relaxed for the time. But the muttering kept on as the men separated. Truth was, by this time our rations were barely enough to keep us alive.

Toward the end of June, a sentry called a warning. Again we swarmed to the parapet, looking in the direction he pointed. Trudging toward us along the path from the village on the east came a small figure. As it approached we discerned a woman burdened with several baskets. On her back was a cradleboard. A young soldier broke into a startled exclamation and hurried to the captain. Evidently permission was granted him and, the gate being opened, he ran to meet the approaching figure. Relieving her of her burdens, he hurried her into the fort.

It was Private McLeod and his Cherokee wife and child. She spoke to him with much gesturing. Meanwhile the baby stared at us from his cradle, his black eyes and tawny cheeks shining with health.

Her message was brief: All the warriors of the river villages had departed to meet the great army that had burned the Lower Cherokee towns and was now on its way to the Middle towns. Great men dressed as women were in the army—a shout arose, "Them's the Highlanders, God bless 'em!"—and they marched with great drums and bags from which came fearful noises as of animals squealing. Even louder shouts broke into the narrative: "Them's the bagpipes!" McLeod's wife had come to bring her husband food and to take refuge from the approaching army, for they were sure to burn all the Overhill villages.

A feeling of elation swept over us at this cheering news. When an experimental sortie was made to test the truth of the reported absence of all the warriors, a warning scattering of shots sent the men running for the safety of the fort. Nevertheless, for the following week we went about our duties in a more cheerful frame of mind.

Abram and I began to talk once more of our friends in the house on Meeting Street.

By July the last of the breadstuff was eaten. Now the horses were butchered. All salt had long ago been used, and the dirt underneath the empty barrels was taken up and washed for its salt content. The ground within the fort was bare of grass—it had disappeared into the stewpots. The shingles and boards of the smithy were being used for fires. Day succeeded day, and we waited in vain for news.

One evening we heard a sudden burst of noise. At the edge of the forest appeared a strange procession— dancing and shouting warriors, carrying aloft two objects.

Captain Stuart yelled in sudden recognition, "Drums! The Highland drums! The drums of Montgomery's Highland Regiment!"

Then began a weird taunting drumbeat. We watched in stricken silence. Suddenly one man, driven beyond endurance, grabbed his musket and fired off a useless shot toward the faraway scene. the dancers melted away, and silence descended.

There was no singing about the campfires that night. Men gathered in small groups and murmured as if to comfort themselves against the unthinkable possibility: Montgomery had been defeated! Abram and I ate our small supper and were silent.

Luke Kraft appeared and touched me on the shoulder. He bent to whisper, "You and Abram is wanted at the captains' quarters." Abram's feet were still tender though healing, and he hobbled at my side. One candle was lit, and the small room seemed to be full with the three men present—the two captains and Mr. Shorey. The door was closed despite the hot night.

137

"Angus," said Captain Demere, "I request of you that which I cannot command."

I was puzzled and looked from one watchful face to another.

"These two gentlemen have been consulted and think that you are entirely capable of accomplishing this which I ask," he continued. "Would you carry a message to Fort Prince George and return with the answer?"

I was stunned.

The captain leaned forward. "We are asking this endeavor of you for several reasons. Many of our older men are quite enfeebled by our reduced rations, while your youth and strength have stood you in good stead. Also, you are an excellent swimmer, and it will be necessary for the messenger to swim three rivers—the Tennessee here and the two rivers near Fort Prince George."

I looked at Abram who was grinning in encouragement. He chuckled and addressed the captain. "Yes, suh, Cap'n, this here boy'll do it. Anybody who'd take on three thieves can take on de whole Cherokee nation!"

I had got my voice now. "Yes, sir, Captain Demere, I'll go."

The captain smiled. "With Abram's unbounded faith in you and with our practical advice, I'm sure you will complete what I ask. Draw up that bench, if you please. This instruction will take some time."

Abram standing behind me, I drew up to the candlelit table and learned of my assignment.

"It is absolutely necessary to learn the truth of General Montgomery's defeat—if indeed there has been a defeat. You must discover that at Fort Prince George and return immediately with the answer. Is that clear?"

"Yes, sir."

138

"You are to speak only to the commanding officer. You will carry no written message, so in case you should be captured you may say that you are a deserter. If that melancholy event should come to pass—the good Lord forbid!—I authorize you to give any information to the Cherokees that they demand."

"Yes, sir."

"I have asked these gentlemen for their advice, and I'm sure that Abram can add valuable details from his recent travels. Stuart, you might begin."

"According to McLeod's wife," said Captain Stuart turning to the large map that lay on the table, "the general had already burned the Lower towns—here— and had moved to attack the Middle towns, which lie here. I am guessing that the army was met by the Cherokee here about Nuquasee. Now, if those drums the Cherokee showed us mean anything, I think we must assume that there has been a battle in which a part at least of Montgomery's forces were beaten."

Captain Demere added dryly, "It is even possible that the good general has ordered a retreat. And if that be so, the whole Cherokee nation is occupied with a truly tremendous victory celebration. For that reason, as I said, we think you have a good chance of getting through. Now as to your route. Captain Stuart has traveled two routes to Prince George and will suggest the one to take."

I moved to a position fronting the map, and Captain Stuart stood behind me, pointing to the various lines. I searched them carefully, knowing that my safety depended on an accurate recollection of them.

"There is but one simple instruction, Angus," he said kindly. "Follow the rivers."

Abram nodded emphatically. "Best advice, best advice, boy!"

139

"As you know, the river just below is the Tennessee. Swim across it at a convenient place outside the fort and travel on the north side of it. At least six villages are on the south side; the seventh village, Tallassee, will be ahead of you on the north. Make a wide circle around it."

Mr. Shorey broke in, "My guess is that all the inhabitants will be gathering at Chota, here in the big bend."

"That was the village you saw on our trip to the council," Captain Stuart reminded me.

"Yes, sir. I remember."

"Beyond the villages the Tennessee comes from the east. Follow it. Smaller streams come in from both sides; continue eastward with the main stream. Here it takes a turn south; follow it until it splits into two branches: one from the southeast and one from the south. Be wary when you come to this branching—there is the village of Nuquasee. Circle it and follow the stream that now flows from directly south; avoid the other. By that time the terrain will be open. It will be safer going to hide by day and travel by night. From there strike directly east across one river flowing south, then when you cross the next, the Keewowee, you are at the fort."

"How many days will it take?" I dared to ask.

"Abram came in four days. It will take you longer."

"When shall I start?"

"Early dawn," replied Captain Demere. "It will be best to travel the first part of the trip through the mountains by day. Stay here and study the map longer, if you like. Abram, you may recall certain landmarks familiar to you."

Mr. Shorey spoke up, "I'll gather some food. Do as the Cherokee do—eat and drink sparingly."

Captain Stuart offered a hunting shirt and left to get it.

140

In the next hour Abram went over the map again with me. Then I was required to reproduce the map from memory.

Captain Stuart's hunting shirt was soft deerskin and, when belted, could hold supplies inside. He also contributed three pairs of moccasins. Since I could not use a fire, two could be worn under my shirt to dry. I took only a knife for protection. The food was provided in a small deerskin pouch.

Thus prepared, I lay in my accustomed place and tried to sleep. I turned and tossed; sleep would not come. Abram was also restless, and now and then he would whisper advice.

"De birds, Angus, de birds!"

"What about the birds?"

"Listen to de birds. They talk to you—they tell lots. When they stop singing suddenlike, there's danger 'bout!"

Then, again. "Angus! Sleep with yo' back against a tree!"

In too short a time Captain Stuart came to rouse me, and we hurried through the darkness to the river gate. Opening it, he offered his hand in a hearty grasp. I slipped out, stripped, wrapped my garments and supplies into a tight ball, and crept into the water. Keeping my burden as much above water as possible, I struck out through the river and climbed the opposite bank. I drew on my clothes and waited a short time until I could see the dim outlines of the undergrowth around me. Across the unseen water at my feet loomed the dim outline of the fort. I thought of its known, and now dear, perimeter! Surely a more apprehensive messenger than I never set out.

I traveled swiftly, at first being on fairly familiar territory,

141

and only became more cautious when I approached the village of Tallassee. It was as Mr. Shorey predicted; only a few old women and small children were about. My heart sank. If the rest of the inhabitants were in Chota, they were there to celebrate victory.

From there my way went along the river to the high mountains, now immediately ahead. From here until I neared the vicinity of the Middle towns I might expect to meet no Cherokee, so I sped on my way with a minimum of caution. Abram had urged me to take a few minutes to rest every other hour, and this I endeavored to do. When darkness fell, I estimated that I had gone some twenty miles. Not fast enough! My legs ached from the unaccustomed effort. I ate a handful of the rations, washing it down with water from the river. Then settling against a tree facing a small clearing, I fell into a half-slumber.

I was up at first light and set out again. My legs protested, but I pushed on, more slowly now because thickets of evergreen impeded my progress. They finally grew so dense and impenetrable that I was forced to walk along the riverbanks, every now and then getting soaked. By night I was chilled and exhausted. My handful of food revived me, however, and I slept soundly, rousing occasionally to hear snarls and grunts of large animals.

The next day's travel was for a long way through an extraordinary forest of huge, dark trees. Their tall tops moved in the sunlight high above, and in the green half-light below their large trunks appeared as columns of a great cathedral. The floor of the forest was soft and resinous with their needles.

The river was my guide—rocky, plunging, and now appearing in large deep pools, then falling in stairsteps of cascades. It flowed to the west against my progress east. The air was cool and smelled of a thousand fragrances.

Four days had gone by, when I came to the turning south of the river. Shortly thereafter appeared the dividing of the stream Captain Stuart had described.

At dusk I made a wide detour around what I took to be the village of Nuquasee. On the wind came smells of burning and occasional nauseous odors that stuck in my throat. I came to a sudden halt. Could these be the smells of the battlefield? I searched the skies—a number of birds were floating on the wind, mounting in lazy circles, then drifting down slowly but with purpose. These were the ravens and vultures feasting!

From that night on, I could not go fast enough. The headwaters of the Tennessee were reached; I turned directly east, begrudging the daylight hours when I hid and speeding on my way by night. I plunged into the next river, not bothering to keep my clothes dry. Horror lent wings to my feet. Crossing the Keewowee, the last river between me and my destination, I came to stand before the palisades of the fort that I had passed in the careless days of the preceding summer. I yelled at the sentry who stared at me as if I were a madman.

"From Fort Loudoun!" I yelled. "A message!" Then I sat on the ground and wept.

The gates burst open, and it seemed the whole garrison swarmed out. A big man scooped me up in his arms and carried me inside the fort. Everyone was yelling in excitement. It began to seem to me irresistibly funny, and with the tears streaming down my cheeks, I started to laugh. When I was put down in front of an officer, I had somewhat better control.

"Are you the commandant, sir?" I asked.

"Yes. Ensign Miln, commanding."

143

"Captain Demere's compliments, sir, and he wants some intelligence of General Montgomery's whereabouts and intentions."

A sudden silence descended. Ensign Miln seemed to have difficulty answering me. I looked about. Eyes fell before mine. Then it came to me—there would be no relief!

"General Montgomery . . . " The commandant started again, "General Montgomery has returned to Charles Town, where he is taking a ship to return to New York."

As through a fog I heard the commandant faintly. He explained at length that the army had fought a great battle in which many were killed and more wounded. He spoke of the general's decision to proceed no farther for fear of more fatalities, of his return to Charles Town, and of his decision to sail for New York, claiming to have accomplished his mission of chastising the Cherokees as he was commanded to do.

The British army had retreated. There would be no relief for Fort Loudoun! We had been abandoned!

A groan was wrenched from me, as if I had been struck, as indeed I had, and the big soldier stepped to my side and assured the officer he would feed me and look after me.

My filthy clothes were stripped off, and I was put down in a warm, soapy tub of water and scrubbed and dried and rolled in a clean blanket. Then my large guardian stood over me until I fell asleep.

I must have slept many hours, since I awakened to bright daylight. As I became aware of where I was, the horror of Fort Loudoun's plight swept over me. I hurriedly put on my garments, washed and dried carefully, and ate in preparation for my return trip. Food for the journey was brought, and the commandant insisted that a detail of several soldiers accompany me past Nuquasee. The soldiers knew of a shorter route, running directly to the northwest, that would save me miles. Since the guard accompanied me, we could travel by day, thus speeding my journey. My self-appointed guardian was a part of the detachment, and when we parted the next day, he wrung my hand and begged me to give his compliments to Abram, whom he remembered well.

I felt quite lonely and a great deal calmer and older as I resumed my journey. Now my mind was filled with an aching concern for my friends at the fort, and I could not travel fast enough. I wasted little time in sleeping and rested only when weary beyond endurance. I saw Cherokees only once and avoided them without danger. At the end of the fourth day I swam across the river to the fort, knocked, and was quickly admitted. The sentry took me immediately to the officers' quarters where I stood dripping before Captain Demere, who was alone at the time.

"General Montgomery . . . " I stopped.

"Has been defeated?" he questioned.

"Worse, sir. He has returned to Charles Town and . . . " My voice was shaking.

"And?" prompted the captain gently.

"He and his army have taken ship—for New York!" Tears streamed down my face.

"So, my dear friend," he said, "it's as bad as that!"

I could not answer.

"Are you hungry?" he inquired courteously.

"No, sir."

"Tired?"

"No, sir."

"Nevertheless, you must rest."

As I turned to go he stood, clicked his heels, and bowed.

"Thank you, my friend."

That night Captain Demere told the news to the garrison, commending me publicly for my services. The men, silent now, sat about their small cooking fires. Quiet reigned at the fort, broken only by the calls of the sentries. I had come home, such as it was.

16
Abandoned by God and Man

A mounting anger began to run through the fort, now stunned by the news of General Montgomery's abandonment of Fort Loudoun.

Captain Demere sent for me, and he and Captain Stuart began to compose a carefully worded report to the governor at Charles Town. I cannot remember any of it, except that the captain, in conclusion, stated that the garrison "felt themselves abandoned by God and man."

Abram volunteered to take the dispatch, insisting that his feet were now entirely healed. He was closeted for quite a while with the two captains. When he came out, he was his usual cheerful self. That night he entertained us by singing many songs and concluded with the war chant of his people beaten on the drummer boy's drum.

We lay for a long time before sleep came. He was to leave just before daybreak and was restless too. Finally I could bear in silence no longer the thoughts that crowded in my head.

"Abram!" I whispered. "What did you do it for?"

His voice was amused. He knew what I was asking. "What are you talkin' 'bout, boy?"

"Why did you volunteer to take the message? You've been down that trail too many times already!"

"I was a slave before, boy. You forget that, but me, I never forget! I do what I'm told to do—but now, I's my own man! I do what I want!"

"But, Abram, it's a long and dangerous trail. Let someone else go!"

147

He lay quiet awhile apparently considering this, but when he spoke, I learned he had been thinking of something altogether different.

"Boy, 'member what I tells you. I'm a free man now. I give something for this freedom . . . "

"But you've already earned it! The Assembly rewarded you!"

"Yes, but that was different, boy!"

"How?" I demanded.

"That a reward, what I earned. Now, this a gift."

"A gift?"

"Yes. My old country gone. I never see it no more. This my new country, boy. Lots of folks kind to me. Marse Benn . . . "

"He bought you!"

"Yes, but he never laid no hand on me. He's a kind master."

"Master, still," I insisted.

"Dr. DuPree and Miss Vannie been my friends. You are my friend, boy. Captain Demere, he kind in British-officer way. This my gift to all my friends."

I was silenced.

"You understand, boy?" he asked anxiously.

"No," I said crossly.

Before dawn, the sentry came to call Abram. I went with him to the river gate. In the dim light I saw him take from around his neck a thong from which dangled a small wooden figure. He put it in my hand and said, "For to keep you safe, boy." Then he was gone.

During the morning, Captain Stuart told me that Captain Demere had something for me. When I appeared, the captain gave me a folded paper that Abram had left for me.

I read it, and when I finished, looked at the captain. He

smiled. "Abram dictated it last night and said to give it to you this morning. He was particularly pleased with the legal phraseology."

Abram had attested to his will in which he had appointed me his executor. His one request was that I take the £500 the Assembly had voted him and "buy the freedom of my beloved wife, Tina. It is also my request that my friend, Angus Ferguson, be responsible for her care and well-being." Underneath the words "Abram, his mark" was a large, carefully penned cross.

The men gathered in small groups when off duty to discuss the new turn of events. They did their chores churlishly and with barely repressed mutterings. It was clear that the hitherto strict discipline of the fort was breaking down. The officers went about their duties as smartly as ever; even gaunt and hollow-eyed, they commanded respect more by their example than by their authority as officers. Roll calls showed that a number of soldiers had decided to escape. They were the younger, hardier men. Their going meant a little more corn for the rest of the garrison, but not much.

After several days, when a total of eight men had disappeared, Captain Stuart was busy in the officers' quarters getting some papers in order as I came in the door. He looked up with a smile and gestured to the small, neat pile. "Well, Angus, your duties are almost over—very little paper left, and no more ink."

"Ink's no problem, sir. Besides using soot, I've heard that a very serviceable substitute may be made by pounding the oak galls and dissolving them in water."

"Really? Where did you pick up this bit of information?"

"Mistress Bacon told me."

"That woman is amazing."

I laughed. "She is indeed, sir. I think she counts herself the mother and guardian of the whole fort. Just now, however, she's given up."

"Mistress Bacon!" exclaimed the captain.

"Yes, sir. She said if you or Captain Demere had been commanding Montgomery's army we'd never have been abandoned!"

"Ah, yes—if wishes were horses, beggars might ride! We do appreciate her confidence, however."

"We all feel like that, sir; indeed we do!"

"That brings up a matter that makes strange advice, coming from an officer, Angus, but I feel that since it was my suggestion that you come with us to escape danger in Charles Town—Lord, how long ago that seems!" He paused, then continued, "Captain Demere concurs with this advice as well. How shall I say it? We think you should leave, Angus, and make the best way you can to either Charles Town or Virginia!"

"Desert?" I asked, startled.

"It wouldn't be deserting. You are an employee of Mr. Elliot's, not a soldier."

"But to desert!"

"Angus, listen to me," the captain said. "I've known the Cherokee and other tribes for years. I like them; I respect them. They don't like us or trust us, often for good reason. Think of what this fort means to them! We are behind their mountains!

"And, Angus, do you know—of course you don't— what they do when they torture a prisoner? Angus, I beg of you, leave this condemned place!"

My throat was dry. I was shaking. The smells of the battlefield at Nuquasee seemed to be strong in my nostrils. Then a thought struck me. "But you are not deserting!"

150

"I have sworn an oath."

I said the first thing that came in my head. "My father would not desert, I think. And besides"—a new thought occurred to me—"Mistress Bacon needs me. And the children—what will happen to them? Will the Cherokees let them go?"

"I cannot guess."

"Then, sir," I gulped, finding it immensely difficult, "I had better say no."

"Take some time to think it over, Angus."

"No, sir," I declined. He seemed so saddened by my refusal that I tried to explain. "If I thought it over, it would just be more difficult because I want so much to go, sir."

I turned to go, looking back at the captain, who sat staring at the papers.

"I'm sorry," I said.

And, indeed, I often regretted my decision and had all I could do to keep from wandering to the captains' quarters and from telling them that I had decided to take their advice.

It was August now. The noonday heat was terrific. Only the cooler nights made the days bearable. On one of those hot days a large group of thin, shabby, sullen-eyed men came to stand at the open door of the officers' quarters and asked the favor of a hearing with Captain Demere. He came to stand at the doorway, as thin and shabby as any confronting him, but with a lift to his head and an erectness to his carriage.

They had chosen their spokesman well—a slow, rawboned man whose speech had the drawl of the backcountry. He had the grace to remove his hat.

"Yes, Robertson?" the captain inquired.

"Cap'n Demere," Robertson began slowly at first, warming up to his subject. "We've been talking this over, sir, for several days. It's not that we ain't thought it out and what it might come to—but we're asking you to surrender, sir."

He stopped, expecting an answer from the silent figure confronting him. Getting none, he continued uncomfortably, "Sims and Munford and me was elected by the men to bring it to your attention, sir. There ain't no possibility of help since that poor excuse for a general has turned tail and run. Nobody nowheres cares whether we lives or dies, and we're starved and plumb wore out. We're aimin' to pick up and leave."

"You realize this is mutiny?"

"Yes, sir, you might call it that."

A voice from the crowd spoke up, "Cap'n, we ain't goin' against our officers, if that's what it means by mutiny. We ain't had better officers, but we're just weary of sittin' here starvin' and penned up like animals waitin' for slaughter!"

The captain raised his voice to answer. "Have you given any thought to the possibility of death and torture from the Cherokees?"

There was an uncomfortable silence.

Robertson answered, "Yes, sir. We thought of that."

"Your minds are made up, then?"

"I reckon they are, sir."

"Very well, I shall call a council of the officers. You are dismissed."

Early the next morning the officers met and talked for a long time. They were watched through the open door by the men, who stood about in silent groups. I was called to take down the terms suggested. There was some little trouble about the ink, but we found enough dried material left in the pewter containers to mix with a little water and came up with a pale substitute. Captain Demere asked the officers to sign it.

Because it was agreed impractical to maintain the fort any longer, such terms as could be procured from the Cherokees, consistent with honor, were to be accepted and the post abandoned.

It was desired that the garrison should march out with arms and drums, each soldier to have as much powder and ball as the officers should think necessary for the march and what baggage he chose to carry. A number of Cherokees were requested to accompany us to hunt and supply us with meat. As many horses as the Cherokees could conveniently supply were also desired. The great guns, the powder and ball to supply them, and any spare arms were to be delivered to the Cherokees on the day appointed for our abandonment of the fort.

Captain Demere read the suggested terms to the assembled men. They were of intense interest to his hearers and were listened to with close attention.

Captain Stuart and Lieutenant Adamson went off on their mission flying a white flag. They were dressed in all the regimentals and looked very smart, even if the uniforms hung on them as on scarecrows for gauntness.

17
August 10, 1760

The whole garrison was set to putting the fort to rights for our departure. There was considerable grumbling about the necessity of doing so, but "captain's orders!" started the men to work with a will. Each man was released to pack what baggage he found necessary to carry, with the admonition "Keep it light! There's many a mile between here and Charles Town."

Most were only burdened with the clothes on their backs, their muskets and ammunition, and the remainder of the food. Blankets and cooking utensils were taken by some, but such supplies were at a minimum.

The two messengers, now accompanied by an escort of Cherokees, returned late in the day. The escort stayed outside, where they were to camp for the night, as the two officers marched into the fort and delivered the dispatch to the captain. That night after supper Captain Demere reread the terms to us and called off the names of the chiefs who had made their marks for their nation. One name was missing—Attakullakulla's.

Early on the morning of the ninth of August we marched out in good order. There were tears in the soldiers' eyes as the drum beat the last tattoo. As we swung down the path to the south, I turned and viewed the palisades of the fort and the silent cannons looking down. Ball and shot had not brought them down; they had fallen to a more insidious enemy—starvation and, I thought bitterly, the cowardice of a general.

Our escort of warriors was numerous. Only a few

horses had been provided, however, and women and children had been mounted for the long ride.

That night we camped along the banks of Cane Creek. Everyone was tired—we had marched some fifteen miles that day—and no one wanted to go to the trouble of starting fires for the pots. Prodded by the officers, however, several fires were kindled. After so many weeks of near starvation, our shrunken stomachs did not accommodate a great deal more than we had been accustomed to. Nevertheless, with the food we became more animated and joined in the night's prayers with deep thanks.

The officers formed us into a circle with the women and children inside. Guards were posted about the camp, our escorts taking their stations alongside of them.

I was so excited that I gave up the useless effort to sleep and crept to where the captains sat, quiet yet alert. The mists rose out of the creek and crept toward the high valleys. There was a restless movement and an occasional murmur from where the women and children were bedded down. Sentries passed in the darkness, their passing being marked by the sound of metal striking against metal.

Couched in a nest of grass, I fell into a partial slumber, filled with memories of the trail at Nuquasee, the silent vultures circling on lazy wings, and the dreadful odors of the battlefield.

I was suddenly awake. There was no sound in the August dawn. A thin morning mist hung about us, but the shrilling of insects and the occasional twittering of birds, heard all through the night, had ceased. "Listen to de birds," Abram had said. "They talk to you." And they spoke now in their silence of danger!

I leaped to my feet.

"Captain," I called urgently, "the birds are quiet!"

Both captains sprang to their feet, listening intently. A sentry ran to the small hill where we stood.

"Captain, the Cherokees have gone!"

"What!"

"They were there one minute—the next there was nobody. I didn't hear a sound. But they're gone!"

Captain Demere called, "Lieutenant Adamson, get the women up and together; put the children in the middle!" And the two captains sped off.

The next moments were frantic with activity. The children wailed. Men rushed to take positions about the small confines of the camp. Sharp commands echoed around its perimeter. As the mist swirled, our straining eyes seemed to see glints of metal and looming figures. Suddenly came a fearful chorus of yells and screams, swelling and rising ever higher, freezing the blood.

Captain Stuart yelled from my left and Captain Demere from my right, urging the men into a closer formation about the women and children.

"Make every shot count!" came the order. I weighed my tomahawk, my only weapon, and braced myself.

Suddenly the attackers came with thundering gunshots and whining arrows. The fog lifted yet more, and I saw the warriors, stripped and painted. At the front was Tsalohi, pulling back on his bow—that strong bow. I followed his line of sight. His target was the figure of Captain Demere!

Tsalohi meant to bring down the commandant, thus his battle honor would be greater. I drew back my arm, poising my weapon for the throw. Now, if ever, I needed the accuracy that Tsalohi had taught me. And yet—I could not kill my friend. Yelling a warning, I threw down

156

my weapon and flung myself before the captain in time to meet the speeding arrow.

Its tremendous force flung me down. A hot pain seared my shoulder. I looked down stupidly to see a shaft—how carefully Tsalohi made his arrow shafts—protruding there. Then he was astride me, his countenance twisted in fury. He flung down his bow and, snatching a knife from its scabbard at his neck, grasped my hair with one hand and lifted the weapon. Scalped! I was to be scalped with my own knife! I saw the gleam descending and twisted violently to avoid it. Pain from my wound surged through my body. His dark eyes glared into mine, and I waited, glaring in return. Tsalohi hesitated. Amid the yells and screams and shots we were silent, frozen antagonists. Glancing at the knife now held inches above me, mad laughter shook me.

"My gift!" I said and laughed wildly.

He hesitated again and looked at the knife. Then he lowered his arm and stood above me, regarding me impassively. Very deliberately, he knelt and hacked at the shaft of the arrow. A red stream came down from my shoulder as he drew it out. The yells and screams faded in my ears, and I fainted.

I woke to hot sunlight beating down. I was held upright by thongs that bound me to a post. On either side of me were similar posts, continuing in a large circle. To each was bound a soldier. To my right, his blue jacket gone, was Captain Stuart. I did not recognize the man to my left. His face was painted black, and he sagged against the thongs that bound him. When I twisted, trying to ease my arms, the sunlight darkened, and I fainted again.

When I woke next, it was night. A fire blazed in the center of the ring of prisoners. Dark figures outlined against the flames circled, singing rhythmically. At each beat a scorching pain stirred in my shoulder and began to throb in time with the dancers.

"Angus?" called Captain Stuart.

I tried to answer, but no sound came. I tried again, my voice a whisper. "Yes?"

"Stand on your feet. Don't let your knees buckle."

I couldn't see that it mattered. "Why?"

"Your feet will take the weight off your arms. There! That's better, isn't it?"

"Yes."

"We're at Chota."

"How . . . ?"

"How did they bring you here? You'll be surprised— your friend Tsalohi slung you over his shoulder like an old blanket and carried you."

That was odd—very odd! "Why?"

"He must be your friend."

An intense thirst was my uppermost thought. Against the pain and agony of the bonds and against the thunderous rhythm of the dancers, I tried desperately to fix my mind on the events of the past day—or was it days? It had been early morning when we were attacked—now it was night. As well as I could estimate in my confused state, at least twelve hours had passed since the early morning raid at Cane Creek.

The thought of water tortured me. Where was the river that I had knelt to drink from on my journey to the south? The waters had been cool and deep, swirling, swirling. The leaves went round in the dark pool. There had been a pool near my home. It too was dark and deep.

I seemed to hear my father's voice—"Angus, Angus!"

I tried to answer, but my throat was dry. Then I became aware of the chanting and drumming. It was reaching new intensity. Captain Stuart had turned away his face, but in the reflection of the fire I saw a terrible convulsion of his features. Was he also wounded? Surely not, for he was Attakullakulla's friend. No one in all the Cherokee nation would touch him, for Attakullakulla would avenge his death.

It struck me then, Where was the other captain— Captain Demere? I lunged against my bonds, screaming. "Where's the captain? What have they done? Captain Demere! Where is he?"

Captain Stuart looked at me.

I think I went mad. I screamed and yelled. My bonds dug into my arms and body. Finally exhausted, I sagged against them. The vultures of Nuquasee seemed to turn and turn above me, and then they were tearing at my wounded shoulder as a great blackness swallowed me.

The swirling fog and freshness of early morning revived me. My fellow prisoners seemed to be sleeping, even in their tortuous positions. The man on the left was gone. The post stood stark and empty. I groaned and Captain Stuart stirred and turned to look at me. We made no attempt to speak. The fire was now only a low, banked smoulder. A desultory drumming was still going on. Suddenly it stopped in the middle of a beat. The silence was shocking and loud.

An erect, slight figure stood at the circle's edge. It was Attakullakulla. His garments were supple white deerskin, fringed and beaded. Ornaments hung about his neck and shoulders. His gun was in his hand and on his shoulder hung a bow and quiver. From the proud face, sur- mounted by the roach and ceremonial eagle's feather, to the feet clad in white moccasins, he appeared, as he truly was, the peace chief of the proud Cherokee nation!

159

He advanced, and the dancers gave way before him. He came on at his stately pace to stand before Captain Stuart. He raised his voice—a surprisingly deep one for such a slight figure—and looked about inquiringly. Oconostota advanced to stand facing him.

Then, as if in a ritual, Attakullakulla lifted the ornaments from his shoulders and stripped off the white garments. He laid them at Captain Stuart's feet. He added his gun to the offering and, with deliberate hands, the bow and quiver of arrows. Then he stood back, clad only in breechclout and moccasins, retaining his eagle feather and the small medallion the king had given him. The ransom for Captain Stuart had been paid.

Oconostota bowed his head in acknowledgment of the offering, then stepped to the captain's side and struck off the bonds that held him. The prisoner was free.

"Thank you," said the captain. Then he gestured toward me. "I cannot go without this prisoner."

Attakullakulla advanced to stand before me. I struggled erect. Our eyes met. Then he turned and called commandingly, and Tsalohi came to stand before him. He gestured toward me. Tsalohi bowed his head, assenting. The little chief turned to look at me again. What did he possess further to offer for my ransom? He had given all that he had for the captain!

He raised his hand and tore off the eagle feather and laid it at my feet, and then—a deeper stillness, if possible—he lifted the last remaining thong from about his neck and laid at my feet the king's medallion!

Tsalohi stepped to my side and cut my bonds. I would have fallen except for the captain's supporting arm. The captain whispered fiercely in my ear, "Now, Angus, for the honor of Scotland!" So the two of us walked slowly out of the great circle, following Attakullakulla.

18
Escape

Afterward I was never able to recall the events of the following days at the vacant fort where we were taken. If I remembered them at all it was as a blur of pain and fever and horrifying dreams in which I lived again the attack at Cane Creek. The captain told me later that Mr. Johnston, who had been put in Attakullakulla's charge, dug the arrowhead out of my shoulder, and then for days afterward, I lay in a fever.

One night I awoke as if from a deep sleep. I found myself lying on a pallet laid on the floor of the officers' quarters. Bright moonlight streamed into the room from the open door where Captain Stuart sat looking out into the night. There was no sound except for the insects' sleepy chorus and the occasional call of a bird. I turned my head. The room was empty; the furniture, the orderly files, and the papers of the two captains were gone. Nothing was left.

"Where is the other captain?" I asked, but even as the words passed my lips, I knew. "He's dead, isn't he?"

The captain turned his head.

"Yes, Angus."

"Why?"

"I do not know."

"Well, I like it not!"

The captain turned and smiled at me. When he spoke I thought it was my father's voice. "Go to sleep, young Job."

It was morning when I woke again. My careful nurse

brought me a broth which I drank greedily. He fetched Mr. Johnston, who pronounced me well on the road to recovery. I slept again.

My days and nights were confused. Often waking in the cool, dark hours, I lay and attempted to sort out recent events. It seemed to me that the young, careless Angus, who had boarded *The Wanderer* so long ago, was gone and that I was another person altogether—older and wiser and less happy. For now I knew I dwelt in a world where good men died and the cowardly lived on and prospered.

I learned that twenty-four of the soldiers had been killed—the exact number of hostages slain at Fort Prince George—and three women. All the officers save only Captain Stuart had perished. The rest of the garrison— some 120—were made prisoners.

In addition to the captain, the surgeon's mate, and I, Mr. Shorey, too, was in the abandoned fort as a charge of Attakullakulla. Among us, Attakullakulla spoke in English. His wife and family lived now at the fort, having taken possession of the soldiers' quarters. They cooked for us and washed our garments so that the four of us began to resemble our old selves rather than scarecrows.

My arm hung useless at my side, but Mr. Johnston fitted up a harness for it so that I could move about without discomfort. He was hopeful that sensation and usefulness would gradually return. Being one-handed was a clumsy business, I found.

Then one day Oconostota marched into the fort, accompanied by a small escort of his nation. Bits and pieces of uniforms were scattered among them—a cross belt here, a red coat there—but each was now possessed of a gleaming gun.

A conference was held—not a friendly one, I judged

from the gestures that I could plainly see from my vantage point on the steps of the officers' quarters. First, Oconostota stood and gave an impassioned talk, then Attakullakulla answered him in a quieter voice and with more restrained gestures.

Captain Stuart next arose and spoke courteously. More talks followed; the voices droned on, and I nodded in the sunlight.

Mr. Shorey's touch and urgent voice wakened me, "Angus, we need you to write a letter! The captain thinks he knows where there is a sheet or two of paper. I'll make a quill for you. Can you find some ink? Hurry! Oconostota is edgy as all get-out!"

I hurried to the fires where the stewpots were kept and directed one of the women to find a cup for me; then, stirring soot from the pots and some ashes into a bit of water, I made an ink of sorts. By that time the quill and papers were found, and I settled myself in front of our captors. The ground served as table, and Mr. Shorey held the paper steady.

Oconostota dictated, and Mr. Shorey translated.

"To the officer commanding Fort Prince George: This is to acquaint you with the bad news that Captain Demere is killed and twenty-four of his command. Captain Stuart and all the rest of the men are saved to manage the great guns"—In my surprise I raised my eyes to Captain Stuart's. He frowned and shook his head—"It will be well for you if you run away in the night."

Each one of the chiefs made his mark. Oconostota demanded that his title, the Great Warrior, be written in English, so that all should remember his reputation. The letter was folded and given to his keeping. Then the delegation strode away.

We stood watching them leave. Then, as if by a

common impulse, we turned and looked at the dark cannons silent on the bastions.

The captain turned to Attakullakulla. "My friend," he said. "You know that I cannot—I will not—turn these guns against His Majesty's forces. It is impossible to think of."

"Oconostota threatened to burn the prisoners before your face if you refuse."

"Even if they compel me," said Captain Stuart.

The chief sighed. "I know," he said.

We sat about the fire and ate our supper in silence, each lost in his own thoughts. Finally, Attakullakulla drew out his pipe and, filling it with the fragrant tobacco, lighted it with a coal from the fire. Blowing it in ceremonial acknowledgment to the four points of the compass, he handed it to the captain. When I would have passed it on, Attakullakulla stopped me by a gesture.

"For you, our youngest warrior!"

"Warrior?"

"Not all bravery is in fighting. You offered yourself to shield the dark captain."

"But I failed!"

"The Great Kanati gives victory. He asks only that we try."

As imperturbably as I could, I drew in a breath of the smoke and, with shaking hand, passed on the warrior's pipe.

When the women had retired from their duties, Mr. Shorey began a rambling account of the building of the fort and the many trials of the endeavor and of how the guns were brought over the mountains.

Captain Stuart looked up sharply. "That's it!" he said in great excitement. "There is the solution!"

"What?" Mr. Shorey asked.

"There are only two men left who know how to get those guns over the mountains!"

"Yes!" Mr. Shorey answered. "A fellow named Taggart and Isaac Lewis."

"Are they still alive?" demanded the captain.

"We can find out tomorrow," said Attakullakulla.

"There it is," said the captain. "They and I are the only ones who know how the guns can be managed. If we are gone, Oconostota will not know how to get the cannons to Fort Prince George. Bring the men to join us here, my friend, and then we must try for the Virginia settlements! How, I do not know."

Attakullakulla sat in silence, his eyes shining in the firelight. The rest of us watched him with sudden hope. Then he turned to the captain. A rare smile lit his face. "Do not you feel the need of a deer hunt? It seems that my friend is hungry and needs his favorite food! I shall so inform the chiefs. We will go with the two you spoke of."

"What if we are pursued?" asked the captain.

Attakullakulla shrugged. "We shall travel fast." Again the smile lit his face. "We shall be very hungry!"

Shouts of laughter startled the night birds, and the men sat long into the night, planning the escape.

The captain waked me in the early morning. "Angus, the chief and I are traveling to Chota to talk to the prisoners. We will take you, the doctor, and Mr. Shorey to Virginia. Will you be able to go with us?"

"Yes, sir!"

"It will be dangerous to leave any here. The chiefs might take out their anger on any left behind. Tell Mr. Johnston. We travel light!"

The surgeon's mate trembled when I told him our plans. The women were asked to prepare food for the trail. There was very little that Mr. Shorey needed to prepare, other than to secure a second pair of moccasins. Mr. Johnston got his small store of herbs and medicines and was ready to travel. He dressed my shoulder, as he did every day, and even though it was still draining, he considered its healing progress satisfactory. He constructed a small, soft bolster of sorts that fitted under the arm and then bound it to my side to make easier going.

It was wonderful to feel so gay again! Now hope lay ahead, and each of us thought of what the next days would bring. Freedom and Charles Town for me!

The following day the captain and Attakullakulla returned, bringing with them Lewis and Taggart, who until then had not been informed of our destination, so cautious was Attakullakulla of alerting the chiefs to our plot. Two other young Cherokees came also. In the rear of the small procession came my friend, Tsalohi, with Attakullakulla's medallion shining on his breast. He had been told by Attakullakulla of our plans and was to go with us to Virginia.

He came to stand before me, smiling. Now my curiosity could be satisfied. I called to Mr. Shorey and he came.

"Mr. Shorey, please ask Tsalohi why he didn't kill me when he had the chance?"

Tsalohi considered the question silently, and we all waited for his answer.

"When I saw the face of my enemy, it was the face of my friend."

Everyone nodded. It was a reasonable answer, and it would have to do me. Then a sly grin appeared on his face, and he added something else. Mr. Shorey was convulsed with laughter, and Tsalohi looked pleased with himself.

"He says," Mr. Shorey gasped, "that it is not proper to scalp a man with his own knife!"

Everyone broke out into shouts of laughter, but I failed

to see the humor of it. I could still feel Tsalohi's tug on my head.

We left in the early hours of a warm September day. We swam the river in darkness, our clothes drying quickly. Our way led to the northeast, to the Great Valley of Virginia.

The going was difficult, for our guide avoided the well-worn warrior's path. Our way, instead, ran along the river valleys where we were much impeded by fallen trees and occasional swamps.

Attakullakulla led with the captain, the surgeon's mate, and me on his heels. Some distance intervened; then came two Cherokees and Mr. Shorey. The rear guard was made up of Lewis and Taggart followed by Tsalohi.

We kept up a steady pace. On the few stops permitted the first day, I would sink to the ground, exhausted. At the captain's anxious glance when we resumed our travels, I would shake my head and struggle to my feet. I had already determined that I should not impede the journey in any way. How I should survive alone in this wilderness I knew not. Others had done it, so I had heard, and so could I.

The second day was no easier than the first, but from then on I was a bit stronger with each day. The awkwardness of going one-armed occasioned many a fall. Mr. Johnston examined my shoulder each night and professed himself pleased.

We gradually drew away from the mountains towering to the south. Now to the north we observed other mountains.

Mr. Shorey gestured toward them.

"Good hunting beyond them, so I'm told. The Cherokee call it the Dark and Bloody Ground. The

167

Shawnee and northern tribes hunt there too. Even come this far."

I shuddered. I wanted no more arrows singing through the air.

Captain Stuart, the soldiers, the surgeon's mate, and I were not armed, unless one would call an occasional knife among us arms. The Cherokees and Mr. Shorey carried bows and arrows. Our hunting, even so, would have been good if we could have paused. Bears, deer, geese, swan, and turkeys were seen.

We ate our dried rations, not daring the danger of signaling our whereabouts with a fire. There was water in abundance, but the Cherokees drank sparingly, and the rest of us followed their example.

At the end of the fifth day it was judged safe to kindle a fire. We huddled about its unaccustomed warmth while the Cherokees and Mr. Shorey went hunting. They returned with some of the small game that was everywhere abundant.. Our delicious feast was washed down with an aromatic tea of sorts made from the forest herbs.

Now we came into territory where we were more likely to find white men—soldiers, traders, or settlers— venturing far. Mr. Johnston, with growing interest, looked about this teeming land as we traveled. At our night's camp he sat next to the captain.

"I never expected to get out of the fort alive, sir."

The captain smiled. "To tell the truth, neither did I."

The man's voice shook.

"I don't deserve it—better men than I have died . . . "

He could not go on.

"I have the same thoughts, believe me, my dear sir," the captain comforted him.

Mr. Johnston sighed. In the days ahead he stood

straighter. For all his shabby appearance he looked like the gentleman he must once have been. The thought came to me that of all the men in the fort he was the only one who had not mentioned where he came from.

After nine days' traveling we came to a small cabin—it could not be dignified by the name of fort—around which were camped a company of the Virginia soldiers.

They ran to greet our party and accompanied us jubilantly to the camp. They had been sent out to find any intelligence of what had happened to Fort Loudoun.

It was here that Attakullakulla, Tsalohi, and the other Cherokees turned back. Captain Stuart took affectionate leave of the chief, who declined to accompany us further.

"My people need me," he explained. "They did not need me for the war, but they will need me for the peace to come."

We stood watching as they left. An unforgettable chapter in my life had closed.

19
Williamsburg

We were escorted by a detachment of the Virginia soldiers from the small camp until we reached the wide, sandy streets of Williamsburg. Here interested spectators craned to watch our tattered group go by.

"From Fort Loudoun?"

"Yes, all the way from the Cherokee country!"

"Yes! An old chief saved them!"

"It ain't possible!"

Mr. Shorey, Mr. Johnston, and the two soldiers were quartered in a large private house. The captain and I put up at Mr. Cooley's ordinary, a small, tidy lodging that afforded comfortable beds and bounteous meals. Here the governor sent word that he would see Captain Stuart and myself as soon as possible.

The first order of business was to assemble decent clothing. Captain Stuart was soon supplied from the military stores available, and bathed, groomed, and thus outfitted, his military glory dazzled my eyes.

My own outfitting presented a problem. Captain Stuart superintended the business. The kitchen boy was called to assist me, since my arm was still useless. Scrubbed and raw from a good soaping, I was now helped into some garments hastily brought by an attentive and talkative tailor. First came knee breeches of bottle green, then a white ruffled shirt, a neckcloth wound around and tied in an intricate knot, a vest of some colored stuff, and then a matching green jacket reaching to my knees.

"How shall I pay for them?" I asked appalled by all this finery.

The captain laughed, "There speaks the Scotsman! My lad, you are now in my employ, and you will pay for your lodging and these fine feathers by many hours of work as my secretary while we are here."

"Shall I powder the young gentleman's hair, or does he require a wig?" solicitously inquired the tailor.

"Neither powder nor wig," announced the captain gaily. "If there are any ladies at the Governor's Palace, they will much prefer the hair as God made it, for it sorts well with the brown skin of our woodsman."

Indeed, the two of us received flattering attention from the royal governor at our audience in the great palace. There were ladies present also, young and old, but I was so uncomfortable in my fine garments and so distracted by the squeaking of my new shoes that I was silent more often than I spoke.

My first night in the ordinary was a distressing experience. The starched crackling of the white sheets and the creaking of the bed made it impossible for me to compose myself. Finally, I hit on a solution—I arranged a blanket on the hard floor and instantly fell asleep.

Since he was the only surviving officer of Fort Loudoun, Captain Stuart was directed by the governor to make a full report of the siege and capture of the fort. He was to provide a list of the dead and to make recommendations to the governors of Virginia and South Carolina as to the recovery and ransom of the captives. Mr. Johnston and the two soldiers were to report to the officer in charge of the barracks.

Mr. Shorey was sent on several trips to the borders of the Cherokee country to assist any who might yet escape and to aid Attakullakulla in his mission of peace. His reports confirmed the fact that the war party's wrath had cooled.

One day Mr. Shorey brought in three soldiers who had escaped from captivity. We were delighted to see them. Near starvation and considerably the worse for their hard journey, they brought cheering news of Mistress Bacon, still a prisoner. She had been treated well by the Cherokees, who admired her indomitable spirit. Her ransom price, one said with a smile, would be high.

"Have you heard any news of Abram?" I asked.

"None," they replied, and Mr. Shorey also shook his head.

"And what of the plans to attack Fort Prince George?" asked the captain.

"Attakullakulla has persuaded them to abandon the attempt. The war leaders feel that the deaths of the hostages are now avenged, and they will probably soon make the first overtures for peace."

This was cheering news indeed, but the lack of news about Abram made my heart heavy.

One day, escorted by Mr. Shorey, there appeared Tuskeegi-Tahee, head man of Citico, accompanied by two younger warriors—one of them, to my delight, being Tsalohi.

I had last seen Tuskeegi-Tahee at the forge in Mistress Bacon's store where he had demanded the repair of his and his companions' guns. The chief, flanked by his two attendants, was an impressive sight. All three, bronzed and straight, were appropriately attired in their finest garments. Beads, silver ornaments, and feathers added a bright touch to their artillery of knives, guns, bows and quivers. Around Tsalohi's neck hung my ransom, the king's medallion, polished mirror bright. He saw me eyeing it and so far forgot himself as to smile.

Formally, through Mr. Shorey, Tuskeegi-Tahee delivered the message from Attakullakulla: At Nuquasee, the Cherokee nation had agreed to sue for peace. Messengers had been sent to Charles Town and they, themselves, had come to Captain Stuart so that he might speak to the governor at Williamsburg.

It was further requested that the fair captain assume the duties of the royal representative to His Majesty's friends, the Cherokee nation. It was the opinion of all that no man was more beloved by the nation and that none would be more attentive to their interest.

Captain Stuart replied that he would be very happy to serve his friends the Cherokees in that capacity, but that the matter must be considered by the royal governors and then referred to His Majesty. Meanwhile, the most pressing business was the prisoners and their eventual return to Fort Prince George or Charles Town.

Captain Stuart invited the chief and his attendants to dine with him at the Raleigh Tavern before they began their return journey.

At the tavern's common room, we created a sensation. When we sat to supper we had a large audience who kept a respectful distance.

Our visitors appeared oblivious of the stares and gave their attention to the difficulties of dining at the white man's table. They took their food in their fingers and drank the soup directly from the bowls. When offered wine, Tuskeegi-Tahee scorned it after one taste and called for "Rum! Rum!" It was apparently his only English word.

Rum was accordingly brought and consumed in great quantities. The captain wisely cut the supper short, and we bade our guests farewell. They went down the street in quite dignified fashion, reeling only slightly.

Early the next morning Mr. Shorey came with an urgent request for Captain Stuart's presence at the gaol. Our visitors had spent the night within its walls, having disturbed the peace of the city sometime during the night.

There they were, only slightly less dignified than the night before. Tuskeegi-Tahee berated the captain angrily, denouncing the hospitality of His Majesty that had so insulted an ambassador of peace.

Captain Stuart left to go before the magistrate and arrange the release of the prisoners. Mr. Shorey and I sat down to await his return. The Cherokees had been put in a room by themselves. They stood with arms folded across their chests, fierce eyes turned away from us.

I put out my hand in a gesture of friendship to Tsalohi. He did not move. Subdued, I sat and waited in silence.

The captain returned soon with the papers for their release. The gaoler came, opened the barred door, and restored their weapons to them.

Out in the bright sunshine, a few bystanders drew near when they observed the striking figures of the three. There was a small audience when Mr. Shorey translated for Tuskeegi-Tahee.

"The ways of the *Unaka* are past finding out. With one hand they offer the belt of peace, with the other they offer small rooms where we cannot see the sky."

He swept his arm about, to the houses and buildings hemming us in. His voice rose.

"Once it was not so! Once great trees rose here, and deer cropped the grass beneath their shade. Once the red men were chiefs of all the land. Then we asked only of the Great Kanati that he give us the wind for our hunting. But now"—his voice rose to a despairing cry—"out of the east, he has sent a red wind that has shriveled us!"

He strode away, followed by one attendant. Tsalohi

174

paused before me. He confronted me with the same scornful glance with which he had first caught my eye on the Charles Town trading path. He snatched off the king's medallion from around his neck and cast it at my feet. Then, to my astonishment, he spoke in English for the first and last time I ever heard him.

"Take your life again. I wear no honors of the English king!"

Then he, too, followed his friends.

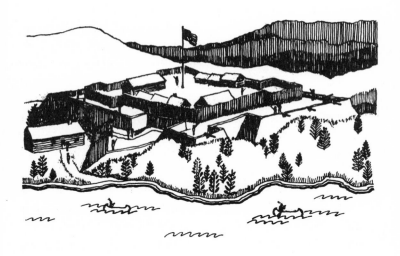

Epilogue

Captain Stuart and I are now awaiting passage on a ship to Charles Town. Mr. Shorey remains to continue his work. Some captives have already been brought to Fort Prince George and others to Charles Town. We have heard that Lieutenant Henry Timberlake has volunteered to go to the Cherokee nation to search for others.

All my thoughts draw me to my friends on Meeting Street. Dr. DuPree's offer of taking me as an apprentice in medicine is kind, and I plan to begin that course of instruction as soon as possible. My obligations to Jamie and to Tina also draw me to the city by the sea. I fear sadly that Abram has perished.

I wear the king's medallion, for it reminds me daily of my friend Tsalohi, of the great chief who gave it as ransom for my life, of Abram, and of the brave men and women who once held Fort Loudoun for the English king.